WITH OPTION TO DIE

With Option to Die

A Captain Heimrich Mystery

BY RICHARD LOCKRIDGE

J. B. LIPPINCOTT COMPANY
Philadelphia   New York

For Hildy

and

for her family

which now is also mine

WITH OPTION TO DIE

I

THE BLACKTOP DRIFTED up a gentle slope, and old maples with spring's young leaves arched over it. At the top of the rise, Eric Martin slowed, then stopped the little sports car and they looked down at the hamlet of North Wellwood. "At any rate," Eric said, "it looks like a peaceful place. A peaceful backwater."

North Wellwood, Town of Wellwood, County of Westchester and State of New York—a village lying in a valley with green hills tumbling around it; a village which was a scattering of houses, most of them white. A white church steeple reached up where the houses clustered most closely. But even there, in what must be the center of the village, the houses seemed lost in trees—seemed to Eric and Ann Martin to be sleeping in the shade of trees.

"Is it really only half an hour from New Canaan?" Ann said. "As Ralph promised. It looks—oh, it looks so far from anywhere, doesn't it? A century from anywhere."

"More," Eric told her, and let the car drift down toward the village. It drifted past a sign: NORTH WELLWOOD. FOUNDED 1706. "Yes, about half an hour. Now that we know the way."

The way had not been hard to find—not really hard to find. "Off the Merritt onto One twenty-three," Ralph Barnes had told them the night before. "Then . . ." Then on this road and that road, and being careful at a certain fork to bear right, not left, since bearing left would lead on to Brewster. "You can't miss it," Barnes had told them the evening before. To that, Eric Martin had said, "Hm-m-m," drawing it out in doubt—a city man's doubt of country roads.

But they had had no real trouble that bright Saturday morning late in May. Route 123 had been easy enough to find. A little more than two miles beyond a sign which proclaimed welcome to New York, the Empire State, there was—as promised by Ralph Barnes— an unassertive road to the left and a sign, almost hidden in a lilac bush, which pointed toward North Wellwood. Some distance farther on they had avoided the branch marked BREWSTER, 10 MI. and borne right on what was, without assurance of any special destination, "South Lane."

Now, having looked down at the village in which they might—or might not—spend the summer, they rolled downhill toward it, looking for Main Street and the traffic light. Cross Main Street and turn right at the next road. That will be Hayride Lane. Then . . .

As promised, it was Hayride Lane.

("Fifth house on your right," Ralph Barnes had said.)

("If you don't count the house on the corner," Lucile Barnes had added. "Because that's on South Lane, really.")

They drove slowly on Hayride Lane. They passed, on the left, a mailbox lettered "Walter Brinkley" and, on the right, one with the name "Powers" printed on it. They went on for a mile or so before they came to a mailbox named "Barnes" and, beyond it, turned into a smoothly graveled drive. The drive curved up, for a hundred yards or so, to a square white house with small latticed windows which seemed to squint down the driveway. The house stood in an acre or more of lawn, which rather needed cutting. There was a big maple tree on either side of the square house and a hemlock hedge ran in front of it, with a break at the doorway. Midmorning sun was bright on the house.

They let themselves into the house. It was bigger than they needed. The rent Barnes had named was even more surprisingly low when one saw the so-big house. Eric, who was only beginning to know a new wife's friends, wondered what was wrong with the house.

Except for the size there was nothing perceptibly wrong with it. There were more rooms than they needed. "We can have people up," Ann said. "We owe everybody." To which Eric, seeking a door which might lead to a basement and heating equipment, said, "Hm-m-m," the sound absent-minded. Not that, in all likelihood, they were going to need heating equipment. Still—half an hour from New Canaan and Hurst Electronics.

"Looks in good enough shape," Eric said, when he had climbed back from the basement. "Not that I know anything about oil burners."

Ann said, "Nonsense. Of course you do, dear."

An electrical engineer, up to the design of the most intricate and inexplicable gadgets, must know much about anything in which electricity is involved. Ann Martin was sure of that. Hurst Electronics happened, at that time, to be under contract to supply the Navy with advanced, and to a degree experimental, sonar equipment.

Eric Martin was, unhurriedly, growing accustomed to the workings of his wife's mind. He grinned at her. He said, "Sonar and oil burners aren't close relatives, darling."

"Electricity is in both of them," Ann told him. "The furniture is all right, isn't it? We can move things around, of course. That sofa sticks out." She pointed at the sofa which stuck out. "And it is only half an hour from New Canaan?"

"Roughly. And not too far from New York, come to that. You'd think they'd keep it for weekends. They don't, I take it, need the money."

"Ralph and Father were the closest friends," Ann said. "When I was little, I called him Uncle Ralph. That, and their being tired of the country, I suppose. No, not the money. Heavens, no."

Eric said, "Hm-m-m," to that. Caution is abandoned slowly.

"Actually," Ann said, "it's almost precisely what we've been looking for. Isn't it?"

Eric said, "Well-l-l," which was an advance over "Hm-m-m."

"Isn't it?"

"You like it, don't you?"

"Yes."

"Then . . . yes."

"So," Ann said, "let's call them up and tell them Yes. Because somebody might come along and buy it out from under us. Did you notice where the telephone is?"

He had noticed. There were three telephones: one in the downstairs hall; two in upper rooms. One of those upstairs was in a room with a desk and bookshelves, and with room in the bookshelves for

[11]

books which cluttered, were stacked in, Ann's little apartment—for six months now *their* little apartment. But the telephone would, of course, be disconnected. Out of service since the Barneses moved, the autumn before, to the apartment in New York. When people left country houses for the winter they turned everything off, including telephones.

Ann was near a light switch. She flicked it up and light went on—went on in two lamps. Ann, understandably, said "Ha!" She went to the telephone in the hall and took the receiver off and listened to it. It buzzed at her. She spun the dial—spun it eleven times, as was required. Which was, she thought as she waited, doing the telephone company's work for it.

Ralph Barnes was glad they liked the house. Glad he had been right about the distance from New Canaan. Did the grass need cutting?

"Sort of."

"I'll give Mike a ring," Ralph Barnes said, from his apartment in New York. "The grass grew on my time. And . . . yes, dear?"

Lucile's voice was just audible.

Ralph said, "All right, I'll tell her," and then, into the mouthpiece again, "Lucile says there are sheets and things—to start, anyway—in the closet at the head of the stairs. Chances are, if I can get hold of him, Mike will be around this afternoon."

Ann and Eric Martin had been married six months that Saturday. They had known each other less than a year. That March Hurst Electronics had decided to move from Long Island City to the vicinity of New Canaan, Connecticut. Eric was part of Hurst Electronics—since March a baffled part.

From Manhattan to Long Island City in the mornings, and back from it in the late afternoons, had not been arduous. One reversed the commuters' field.

Manhattan to New Canaan and back again was another matter. The New Haven Railroad, which is geared for very little, is not geared at all for those who invert the natural order of things. Morning locals, bound reluctantly for Stamford and the New Canaan connection there, creep from the lower level of Grand Central and idle east, stopping whenever opportunity is presented and now and then when it is not. In the evening there are a few expresses inbound but they are not entirely to be relied on. The trip from New Haven to Stamford is one on which almost anything can happen and it is one the express trains make.

Ann and Eric read real-estate advertisements. They went to look at houses offered in the New Canaan area and near it. But those they liked were for sale only, and for the most part at prices higher than they could manage.

(They agreed on this and agreed quickly and neither admitted to the other, or to himself, that quick rejection was only partly based on asking prices. For many there is a finality about buying a house, and to be final one must be sure. Sureness is still, in early marriage, a thing to be searched for, felt and talked toward.)

They had camped out in the apartment which was barely large enough for Ann alone. They had bumped together in it, but that was fine. They had, of necessity, learned closeness, and that was fine too. But it was still a chore for Eric to get to New Canaan and back from it. Camping out is a temporary expedient.

But they had gone to the Barneses' apartment on a Friday evening in May not with any idea of finding a house there. They had gone to have dinner with friends Ann had known since childhood; a man and woman who had watched her grow up, and with whose children she had grown up. The availability of a house in a place called North Wellwood had not been anticipated.

They had been late in getting to the big Barnes apartment on the upper East Side because Eric's express had been late in getting to Stamford from New Haven and even later in reaching Grand Central. Apologies had been offered, together with explanations; and Eric, before cocktails soothed him, had extended the explanations to some length. Commuters on the New York, New Haven and Hartford are inclined to be discursive before they become to a degree resigned. It was new and bitter to Eric Martin. He was a thin, dark man, and on occasion an intense one. The New Haven brings out any intensity which is latent.

[13]

The second cocktail dissolved intensity. Eric Martin said he was sorry he had got steamed up; he said that it was not their problem. It was then that Ralph and Lucile Barnes looked briefly at each other and nodded their heads. Ann noticed the wordless exchange. It was a way the Barneses had with each other—an easy way. Eric and I will find such a way, she thought, and looked at her husband and thought how tired he looked.

It was after dinner that Ralph and Lucile Barnes put their unspoken agreement into words, and the words had to do with a house in a place called North Wellwood; a place half an hour's drive from New Canaan, at any rate in summer. A little longer in winter, but New York State kept its roads passable. And Mike was faithful with his plow on the driveway.

It was a house the Barneses had decided to give up. "A house," Ralph Barnes said after dinner, "gets to be a responsibility as one gets along."

He was, Ann knew, just over sixty. Lucile was several years younger. Neither of them looked as if he was getting along to any marked degree. However . . .

"We've put it on the market," Barnes said. "Just recently. No real nibbles yet. If you two . . ."

If they wanted to rent it through September it was theirs for a figure which brought a "hm-m-m" from Eric.

It was apparent on Monday that Mike, with his mower, had been got hold of. Ann Martin, alone in it, turned a heavily loaded station wagon into the drive at a little after eleven in the morning. The lawn, which had been shaggy, lay smooth around the square white house—smooth and very green. April had brought rain, to the pleased surprise of all the area's inhabitants, who were keeping their fingers crossed. Perhaps a six-year drought had finally been broken.

Ann stopped the wagon just off the road and walked back to the mailbox, because the signal flag was up. She had not lived in the country since she was a little girl—since the Barneses and the Langleys had big Long Island houses a few hundred yards apart, with a hedge between them. There had been a gap in the hedge wide

[14]

enough for the passage back and forth of children named Barnes and a small red-haired girl named Ann Langley. Twenty years ago, that had been, and the girl named Langley had been seven.

A raised flag arm on a mailbox had meant something. That she remembered as she walked toward the box lettered BARNES. (MARTIN would have to be lettered above it.) There could hardly be mail in the box. The raised flag must mean something else. They had, on Saturday, made it to the North Wellwood post office before it closed at noon. They had filled out change-of-address cards and explained to the clerk that any mail addressed to Mr. and Mrs. Eric Martin or —which might make it a little confusing—Miss Ann Langley was to be left in the Barneses' box. But nothing could yet have come of that.

She snapped the box open and a mimeographed sheet lay flatly in it. The sheet was not addressed to anybody. She took it out—after all, one rented a mailbox and its contents with a house—and carried it back to the car and tucked it in the seat, unread. She drove on, and up, to the square white house which squinted at her through sun-brightened windows.

She was not to unload any of the heavy stuff; the bigger suitcases into which they had spent Sunday cramming clothes and certain books—and a picture or two of which Ann was especially fond, and the big, rough bath towels Eric liked and a Chemex for coffee making (the Barneses had used a percolator) and a traveling clock without which Ann had not, for years, gone anywhere and some flat silver which had been Eric's mother's. They had also brought Ann's portable typewriter and both their tennis rackets and Eric's golf clubs, and extra sheets and pillow cases and the electric blanket which, incomprehensibly to Ann, Eric insisted on sleeping under, and two flower vases, in case perennials popped up around the house. (And were recognized by city dwellers.) And a few essential bottles. And bread and sandwich meat and coffee to bridge them over.

"Leave the heavy stuff in the wagon," Eric had said early that morning, before he took off in the sports car for New Canaan and Hurst Electronics. "You hear me? I'll get things in when I get there."

[15]

ever, the manuscript might be expected, had confirmed his mounting trepidation. "Six hundred and thirty-seven?" the publisher had said. "Ouch, Walter."

Brinkley turned over the page which had contained the anecdote and fitted it evenly on top of a sizable pile of pages. He ran down the next page, page 403. He was back on the sound of *r*, as in "draw*r*ing." There did not seem to be anything which could be cut on page 403.

I've been at it long enough for today, Walter Brinkley thought. At seventy, the mind tires easily. Eight-thirty in the morning to —— He looked at his watch. Twelve-thirty. Quite long enough, Walter Brinkley thought, and took his reading glasses off and put them on page 403 to mark it. He then bounced up from his desk and went to his office door and opened it.

He was in time to hear Harry breaking ice out of a tray. Sounds carried well in the white house on Hayride Lane, in the hamlet of North Wellwood. Brinkley said, "Good morning, Harry," down the stairs and Harry Washington said, "Good morning, Professor," back up them. They had met at breakfast, and said "Good morning" then, but what is said at breakfast has no significance.

Now, on hearing "Good morning, Professor," Walter Brinkley was perturbed. Harry was out of character, which might mean he was brooding over something. In character, as part of the game the two men played together, Harry said, " 'Mawnin', Professor." Or, on occasion, " 'Mawnin', suh." Now and then he said, "You-all ready, suh?", which was perhaps overdoing it.

Harry's rendition of the Southern Negro—and Southern white, for that matter—pronunciation was not especially good. He was, to Brinkley's ear, inclined to mix Georgia and Tennessee, as any man born and educated in South Jersey reasonably may. But Brinkley had never mentioned this to his old family retainer from the deepest South. They both enjoyed the masquerade. Only when circumstances were serious, or adverse, did Harry abandon it.

For some months now, Harry had increasingly slipped out of his role. But for some months, and not only to Harry Washington, things had been going amiss in North Wellwood. He and Harry had not discussed it much, but things were not going in North Well-wood as, placidly, they had gone for years. They had talked, when they talked at all of such matters, of the way things were going in those years of violence throughout the nation. That one of them was pink-faced and very white-haired and the other tall and thin and middling-brown did not enter into what they thought and said.

Perturbed now, Walter Brinkley bounced downstairs. Harry, his white jacket as immaculate as always, was by the terrace door, waiting to open it. He held a tray in his left hand. There was a little pitcher on it, the pitcher filled with ice and pale liquid. On the tray, also, there was a thin-stemmed cocktail glass, with crushed ice pressed down in its bowl. Ritual held, if charade did not. Harry opened the door for his employer, and Walter Brinkley went out onto the terrace and to a table in the shade. The May sun was warm that Monday mid-day.

Harry emptied crushed ice from the cocktail glass onto the lawn, which still, for all the previous month's rainfall, could take whatever moisture came its way. He poured martini into the glass and twisted lemon peel over it and rubbed the twisted peel around the edge of the glass. He put the peel in an ash tray at the far end of the terrace, and returned to stand in front of Professor Walter Brinkley and to ask him, still in the speech of South Jersey, if shirred eggs and sausages would be satisfactory. He actually said "satisfactory" and Brinkley was more than ever perturbed.

Brinkley sipped from his glass. The martini was, as always, perfect.

"All right, Harry," Brinkley said. "What is it?"

"Mr. Peters was shot last night," Harry Washington said. "Mr. Thomas Peters. A flesh wound, I understand. Nothing serious. Accidentally, he insists. Some kid with a new rifle, shooting at a target and missing it. It happened before, Mr. Peters says. About a week ago. Then he wasn't hit. But he was near a tree on his place and the bullet hit the tree."

"That's not good," Walter Brinkley said. Then he said, "Sit down, Harry, and tell me about it."

There was nothing unusual in the suggestion nor would there

have been in a further suggestion that Harry make himself a drink before he sat. Two men who live together in a too large house are not, if they like each other, inclined to adhere strictly to formalities. Harry often sat with his employer when invited, and drank with him, too. And at such times he stepped out of his role as old family retainer.

Brinkley did not then suggest the drink that day because, on being invited to sit down, Harry Washington stood very erect and shook his head.

"No, Doctor," Harry said. "The terrace is in sight from the road."

There were two things wrong with that. Brinkley was entitled to be called "Doctor," by virtue of his Ph.D. He did not much approve of the appellation, which made much of what, in his world, was too common to convey any distinction. Almost never before had Harry Washington put "Doctor" before his employer's name. It was now as if he put a fence between them.

The other thing wrong with what Harry had said was that Brinkley knew perfectly well the terrace was in sight from the road and could not, for the life of him, see what difference it made.

After looking up at his employee for several seconds, Brinkley said, "So?"

"Things aren't the way here they've been before," Harry said, and then, "Shirred eggs ought to be cooked slowly, Doctor."

Walter Brinkley knew that shirred eggs ought to be cooked slowly. He also thought they ought not to be cooked too hard.

"There's time enough," Brinkley said. "I may have a second drink, Harry."

"Yes, sir."

"Did Mr. Peters go to the police about it? About this accidental shooting?"

"No. He doesn't want to make an issue of it. The way things are."

"Damn it, man," Brinkley said. "Sit down. You want me to get a crick in the neck looking up?"

Harry said, "Well-l-l," and pulled a chair near, but not really very near, and sat on it. He sat on the edge of it, which was difficult, since it was a small director's chair.

"Anybody," Brinkley thought, "would think you think I was the one who took potshots at Mr. Peters."

"No," Harry said. "Nobody would think that. But somebody did. He knows it. We all know it, Doctor."

There is a certain way of using the word "we." It is a way which excludes others. Brinkley had never heard Harry use it so before; never before so build a fence between two men with a single word. The house they both lived in—Harry in his own apartment on the ground floor—was big, but it was not big enough to hold a fence.

The "we," used as Harry Washington used it, was in a way a declaration, as well as a fence. It explained what had not really needed to be explained about Washington's lapse into unaccented American. (Or, of course, as near as any speech comes to being unaccented.) Harry had lightheartedly, sure of understanding, burlesqued something of which he himself was a part. It could no longer be burlesqued. That game was over.

"Mr. Peters should have gone to the police all the same," Brinkley said.

He realized he was being careful with the "mister" and that Harry knew he was. If Thomas Peters had been a white man, Walter Brinkley would have called him, at any rate in his absence, merely "Peters." He wished he had this time. It was too late now; now Harry had noticed excess courtesy and probably thought it condescension.

"Damn it all," Brinkley said. "Go get yourself a drink."

Harry looked at him for some seconds, and lines of thought, of uncertainty, appeared between his eyebrows. Then, without saying anything, he got up from the chair and went into the house. Whether he would come back with a drink or set about the shirring of eggs was, suddenly, a vital point. Brinkley drank his martini more rapidly, a good deal more rapidly, than he usually drank. He felt uneasiness about many things, including what Harry would do. It's that damn club Peters is organizing, Walter Brinkley thought, and at once realized the thought unfair. The club was merely bringing to a head what had been swelling up in the hamlet of North Wellwood for a long time. Brinkley had lived in North Wellwood most of his life. It was changing under him. The club was only part of the change, but it was a climactic part. He could look back on it as he waited to find out whether Harry was coming back with drinks for both of them.

It had begun with things which seemed to have nothing to do with what it was coming to. (Not that it was possible to say precisely when it had begun.) But the school board business was what had made Walter Brinkley, professor emeritus, first think about it.

It was not primarily that, after two years on it, he and Faith Powers had not been re-elected to the school board. The qualified voters of the Town of Wellwood had a right to decide who was to supervise the education of their children. If they wanted to remove from it the only two qualified educators who had ever been on it, that was their business as voters. If they wanted to use money which would have paid for good teachers to enlarge the gymnasium the matter was one for them to decide. There was no other way Walter Brinkley could think of to run a town or, for that matter, a nation. School-board meetings had taken a good deal of time which he preferred to spend on *A Note on American Regional Accents.*

There had been, in the discussions which preceded the election, in letters to the editor of the North Wellwood *Sentinel,* considerable reference to "so-called liberals." There had been derisive comments on "intellectuals" who were trying to bring "new-fangled" methods into teaching. One letter writer had demanded to be told why children were being taught communism in the North Wellwood High School, and this had been perplexing until it developed that the one-time existence of a man named Karl Marx had been admitted by the instructor of a course on current events.

And, although Brinkley had not learned of this until he and Faith Powers had finished ninth and tenth in a field of ten, there had been reference to the Aaron Nagle case, which Brinkley had supposed buried in the past—buried some ten years deep in the past. He and Faith Powers had both been members of the Dyckman University faculty then, and so had Assistant Professor Aaron Nagle. Nagle turned out to be a member, and a vociferous one, of the American Nazi Party. He made many speeches in which Jews, who were also of course Communists except when they were in complete control of the nation's economy, were the hidden organizers of a Negro conspiracy, the purpose being to destroy Anglo-Saxon civilization.

It was, Brinkley thought, most evil nonsense. But when there were shrill demands that Nagle be fired from the faculty Brinkley had been one of those who defended, not what Nagle said, but his right to say it. They also pointed out that Nagle had not said any of these things in his classes, which would have been a little difficult in any case, since he was an assistant professor of physics. A good many others on the faculty, including Associate Professor Faith Powers, who like Brinkley was a member of the English department, had joined in the defense of academic freedom. Brinkley himself had thought that freedom should be indivisible and hence no more the property of academicians than of anyone else, but had not stressed the point. He had quoted Voltaire—"I disapprove of what you say, but I will defend to the death your right to say it"—on several occasions and perhaps, he thought afterward, a little too frequently.

The situation had been somewhat sticky, since Nagle had had tenure. Nagle himself had resolved it, to the surprise of everyone, by voluntary resignation, tendered in a letter to the trustees of the university. The letter had been long and somewhat rambling, and filled with denunciations of the Communist conspiracy which had led, expectedly, to the violation of his constitutional rights. He had sent copies of the letter to the newspapers, which edited to avoid libel.

The resignation had been accepted with alacrity. Brinkley had almost forgotten the incident until he discovered that those who did not want him and Faith on the Board of Education, Town of Wellwood, had not.

Brinkley had been only a little surprised by his rejection, having long known that gymnasiums are vital to education and that teachers are not. He had been unsurprised, also, when the best teachers of the North Wellwood schools resigned and went elsewhere.

He had been surprised to discover that he was a "so-called liberal,"

[27]

since he had always, like the rest of North Wellwood—and most of the rest of Westchester County—voted Republican. He had been surprised at the violence of feeling which seemed to underlie the entire, and so minor, issue of the school board. He had not supposed that the essential—and, on the whole, gentle—conservatism of the hamlet he had lived his life in was in any manner threatened or that anybody had cause to think it was.

He felt that then, somehow, the mores of the community had begun to change. He supposed now, as he waited for Harry Washington to make up his mind and thought that Harry was taking his time about it, that the attitude of the town had not so much changed as intensified. What the people of the community had taken for granted was now, many of the people thought, threatened. The issues were suddenly, not altogether explicably, tensely drawn. Ralph Barnes's sale of a big house in a good part of town to Thomas Peters, Negro, had beyond doubt, and beyond reason, created tension. And now this matter of ——

Harry came out onto the terrace and carried a tray. On the tray he carried the small martini pitcher and another chilling cocktail glass. He also carried an old-fashioned glass with brown liquid in it. Harry was a bourbon drinker, when he drank at all.

He served Walter Brinkley, carefully, with no comment. He twisted fresh lemon peel over the fresh martini. He sat down with his own drink where he had sat before. But this time he did not sit on the edge of the tippy chair.

"Has Peters had trouble before?" Brinkley asked him, remembering this time to avoid the over-politeness of the "mister."

"Not really trouble," Harry said. "Oh, what you'd expect, I suppose. The man next door—there's more than a hundred yards between them—has put his house up for sale. Peters' mailbox was knocked over a couple of times. His wife thinks she has to wait longer than other people at the market, but that's a thing we're sensitive about—imaginative about. I've never had that trouble." He paused and sipped from his glass. "Until the last few months, anyway," he said. "And I may imagine it."

"Our mailbox has been knocked over," Brinkley said.

[28]

"Yes," Harry said. "On Halloween. Neither time vandals went after Peters' was Halloween. And the second time—that was only a couple of weeks ago, Doctor—they flattened it. As if they had run a truck over it."

"It's the club, isn't it?"

"Part of it's the club," Harry said. "Most of it, I suppose. But there's a different feeling here from what there used to be. You probably haven't noticed it, with your book and all. We didn't have the NAACP dinner this year. We lost money last year."

Harry was a past-president of the local chapter of the National Association for the Advancement of Colored People. Brinkley himself was a member but not, he feared now, a very attentive one. For almost as long as he could remember, the NAACP had given annual dinners in the community room of the Congregational Church. At them, Negroes and whites had eaten together, of expertly fried chicken. The intermingling had perhaps been not much more than a token. It had, at any rate, been that. Local purveyors had supplied frying chickens at cost and sometimes at less than cost.

"I suppose," Harry said, "it's what they call the backlash. I—well, I hadn't thought it would reach this far—to North Wellwood. To such a quiet little place. None of us had. Not that things were very good for us before, of course. Housing for one thing. But now there's animus. Not open, yet. Or people are careful about it. They shoot from behind trees."

There was a bitterness in Harry Washington's voice for a moment. Brinkley had never heard it before. Life had always seemed rather to amuse Harry Washington.

"And," Harry said, "from behind words. You've read this thing from what they call the Preservation Association? Or did you tear it up, Professor?"

Brinkley disliked a littered desk and commonly tore up unread mail which he deduced he did not need to read. All mail addressed to "Boxholder" was so destroyed, unopened. So were letters addressed to "Walter Huntington Brinkley." Brinkley had many years ago discarded his second name, feeling it made him sag in the middle, but it still appeared, in parenthesis, in *Who's Who in*

[29]

America. When the "Huntington" was included, Brinkley knew that the writer had used *Who's Who* as a mailing list, presumably to offer for sale something which Brinkley did not want to buy. It was true he was sometimes impetuous. Once he had torn up his monthly retirement check, but Harry Washington, who kept an eye on such matters, had found the pieces and taped them back together.

"I may have," Brinkley said, with caution. "I don't remember reading anything from a preservation association."

Harry was prepared. He took a folded sheet from the inner pocket of his white jacket and carried it to his employer. "Do you Want THIS Country Club?"

Brinkley had left his reading glasses on his manuscript. He could read quite well without them, until he got a headache. He could read the communication from the North Wellwood Preservation Association without difficulty, although it was single-spaced. The style bothered him considerably, but he could read the words.

He looked up when he had finished and looked at Harry Washington's waiting face.

"Traffic congestion is a bad thing," Walter Brinkley said. "Litter is to be deplored. So is a weasel."

Harry Washington smiled at that. It was the first time Brinkley had seen Harry smile that day. Harry smiled readily, since a good many things amused him. This smile was brief.

"There's a poem I like," Harry said. "By Robert Graves. About cats. Cats, he says, make their point by walking round it. It's all right for cats. For humans, as you say—weaselly. Why don't they come out with it?"

"As you said, Harry. Because they want to hide. Don't want to admit openly what they're getting at. Do you know who they are?"

Harry Washington shook his head. He said people had been guessing. He said, "They say there's a pretty active chapter of the John Birch Society in the town."

"Birchites aren't anti-Negro," Brinkley said. "Not professedly, so far as I know. Just anti-twentieth century."

"They come in all kinds, from what I hear. People do, you know. All kinds of people. Including my kind, Professor. Black power and take over with guns. And we are part of the twentieth century, Professor."

It was the same "we" Harry had used before.

"There's always a lunatic fringe, as they call it," Harry Washington said. "I'd better go fix the eggs, Professor. Unless you'd like another drink?"

He finished his own drink and stood up and waited.

Walter Brinkley was tempted, unexpectedly. He felt disquiet; three martinis before lunch would dissolve disquiet. And me with it probably, Brinkley thought. Walter Brinkley said, "No," to the waiting Harry Washington.

Harry put empty glasses on the little tray and went to shir eggs and broil sausages and Brinkley sat in the shade, and in disquiet, and considered the change, the tension, which had come to the quiet community he was part of. He wished that Thomas Peters had bought his house somewhere else, and planned his club for another locality. It was, he thought, a weasel wish and that it was a very common one. New roads are needed, but not through my property. Equality is to be ardently desired, but not next door. Issues must be joined and, sometimes, sides taken. But preferably in the abstract.

There was, too evidently, not to be anything abstract about the North Wellwood Country Club, particularly if people were going to start shooting at Thomas Peters from, as Harry suggested, behind trees.

While he waited for Harry to come out again and tell him that his lunch was served, Brinkley ran through his mind what he knew about Peters. He had met Peters only once, at a rather large and somewhat ostentatiously unsegregated party, and talked to him only briefly. It had been difficult to talk to Peters that afternoon because so many gathered around to prove to everyone that they drew no color lines. Peters, Brinkley thought, had been wryly amused, probably in part because he was used to it.

Knowing Peters by reputation was another matter. He was prominent as an attorney, practicing in New York and frequently in Washington. He had been active in civil rights cases; had often represented the American Civil Liberties Union when it intervened as *amicus curiae*. He also, a little unexpectedly, had an extensive practice as a corporation lawyer. When he had purchased, from Ralph Barnes, a big house in a good part of North Wellwood, the *Sentinel* had made a front-page story of it, noting the arrival of a "distinguished new resident." But, of course, Clayton Foster was always a man to stick his neck out.

He probably, Brinkley thought, will stick his neck out on this. I hope not into a noose. Publishing a small-town weekly can be a precarious occupation.

As, evidently, could the promotion, as head of the corporation, of a country club which was not only a traffic menace and a source of "litter" but interracial. That was the point the Preservation Association had weaseled its way around.

In Westchester County, State of New York, it would, Brinkley thought, be quite a point. He doubted if it was one which had ever been raised before and, summoned, went in to eat shirred eggs and sausages.

The eggs were, as always, precisely as he liked them. They were the first things—except the martinis—which, on that bright May day, had been.

III

THE MAPLES INN stretched itself along Main Street, across from the Congregational Church. It was the white spire of the Congregational Church which one first saw on looking down into the gentle valley in which the hamlet of North Wellwood nestled among its trees. The inn was close to the street, which had once, Ann thought, been a narrow road, a dusty road or a muddy road. Beside the door of the inn there was a small sign, fixed to ancient clapboard. AN INN SINCE 1792 the sign read.

Ann had followed the bright blue Mercedes to the inn—followed it along Hayride Lane in the big, by comparison sluggish, station wagon and had honked acknowledgment when Faith Powers gestured toward her own house; had followed it as it jogged into South Lane and right-turned, the lights favoring, on Main Street. She had followed it into the parking lot of the Maples Inn.

She had not expected to do any of these things. She had expected to have a solitary drink and a sandwich in the kitchen. She had been taken under a brisk, small wing.

Ann had offered Faith Powers a second glass of Dubonnet and, with that refused, suggested she make them sandwiches. She was told that she had enough to do without having a guest for lunch the moment she arrived. She was told that Faith Powers had a better idea.

"You'll have to go into the village to market anyway, I expect," Faith said when a sandwich was offered. "Unless you brought things with you? To feed him with."

Ann had planned to market.

"Then we'll have a bite at the inn," Faith told her. "Sally Lambert's got a quite good chef. Then I'll guide you to the supermarket I use. It's in a back street, rather."

"Only," Ann said, "there are things I ought . . ."

[33]

She was told she had done enough for one day, and that not everything could be done in one day. She had, Faith told her, driven up from New York and lugged things into the house and probably made up beds and . . .

"You'll be better for a break," Faith told her, and Faith was firm. Not authoritative, but firm. She had been asked to welcome; she intended to welcome. When she had something to do, Ann thought, Faith Powers put herself briskly into it.

Ann had felt no need to be guided or protected. Nor had she supposed that North Wellwood would be, for herself and Eric, more than a quiet place to spend the summer while they continued to learn about each other. A retreat for two; that was what it was to be—was to have been. Certainly the proposed country club, interracial or not, would have nothing to do with them. They would live detached. The tempest, and it was clear from what Faith told her over their first drink that there was a tempest in this apparently tranquil teacup, would blow around them, leaving them unbuffeted.

Two things moved her to say she was tempted by the thought of leisurely—but not too leisurely—lunch at the Maples Inn. One was that she was more tired than she had realized before she had sat down to her drink. The other thing was, quite simply, curiosity. It was part of her trade as an interviewer for the network to be curious.

"The inn is usually busy for lunch on Mondays," Faith told her. "So many places close on Mondays. You'll meet quite a few of your new neighbors, I expect."

"I don't imagine we'll ——"

She stopped because Faith Powers was smiling at her and at the same time shaking her head.

"Communities like this are sponges," Faith Powers said. "They suck you in. And they can squeeze you out, Mrs. Martin. This one squeezed Lucile and Ralph out, in a way. They didn't tell you that, did they?"

"No."

"I gathered that from Lucile. They've talked it over, apparently.

[34]

Had second thoughts. Probably it won't come to concern you and your husband. But —— Shall we go and have lunch?"

Ann moved the station wagon so the bright blue Mercedes could spurt past it. She followed the spurting sports car to the parking lot of the Maples Inn, which was reasonably full, and pulled in beside it. They walked around the corner of the long, low building. A two-story building, probably with low ceilings, certainly with small windows, tight against winters of long ago. It had been recently painted and was very white with the early afternoon sun on it. Under this new coat of white, Ann thought, generations of paint are encrusted.

The entrance hall of the Maples Inn was a low-ceilinged oblong, with a flight of stairs rising from the end of it, with a doorway on either sidewall at the bottom of the stairs. A tall, thin woman with gray hair pulled tightly back stood between the doorways. The sound of voices, and apparently of a good many voices, came through both doorways. A smile dented the long face of the gray-haired woman as Ann and Faith Powers went into the entrance hall.

" 'Morning, Sally," Faith said. "Brought you a new customer. Mrs. Martin. This is Sally Lambert, Mrs. Martin. Mr. and Mrs. Martin have taken the Barnes place for the summer."

"I heard they had," Sally Lambert said, and then, to Ann, "I do hope you'll like it here, Mrs. Martin."

She had a dry voice and spoke quickly.

Ann was sure she would like it there.

Mrs. Lambert led them through one of the doorways into a long, again low-ceilinged, room with most of one side of it a fireplace. There was a table set for four across from the fireplace and Mrs. Lambert stopped in front of it and said, "Tony." A waiter in a waiter's black jacket, wearing a waiter's black bow tie, came through a doorway which connected the long room with a corridor bar and pulled the table out so they could sit behind it and said, "Good morning, Mrs. Powers. Ma'am."

"This is Mrs. Martin, Tony," Faith Powers said. "I want you to take care of her. We're both having Dubonnet on the ——" She

[35]

paused and looked at Ann, who nodded. "Rocks. And tell Adam we want the blond kind."

To which the waiter said, "Mrs. Martin" and "I'll tell him, Mrs. Powers" and took two outside place settings off the table and carried them away.

There were tables at the end of the room and, beyond the entrance to the bar corridor, others along the side opposite the fireplace, which was enormous and blackened and looked as if fires had burned in it for many years.

"This is the original part," Faith Powers said. "Built before the Revolution. Nobody knows when exactly. The Bennington place it was then. There are still a good many Benningtons around these parts. The other wing is quite new, by comparison. Around 1800, Mrs. Lambert thinks. Somebody carved a date in one of the beams and ——"

Somewhat abruptly she quit speaking, although Ann had listened, turning to face her. Now Faith Powers looked beyond Ann toward the end of the room and her white eyebrows drew a little together. There was intentness on her round, pink face. Her blue eyes narrowed.

Ann turned and looked in the direction her companion looked.

There were two tables at the end of the long room, and two men were sitting at each. Of the two at whom Faith seemed to be looking most intently, one was narrow-shouldered and dark-haired. His face was long and his nose narrow and emphatic. The other man, younger and considerably wider, had a square face and a cleft chin and wide-set blue eyes under a rather low forehead. His hair was a blond brush.

Both men were drinking coffee. The dark man lifted a metal pot and gestured with it toward the other's cup and the blond man put a shielding hand over his cup and shook his head. Then the dark, slight man pushed the table away from them and started to get up.

Faith twisted in her chair then and half stood so she could look through a grating behind their table and into the bar. She stayed so until the two men, the blond almost a head taller than the other, had passed the table and gone out into the entrance hall. Then she sat down again and turned to Ann and smiled at her and said, "Adam's a dear. But he sometimes takes forever. He's pouring them now."

Ann nodded her head, to show she listened.

"I'm sorry, dear," Faith said. "For a moment I thought one of them was somebody I knew. A long time ago. But it wasn't, of course. What was I saying?"

"That somebody had carved a date in a beam," Ann told her.

"Of course. They were making changes in the main dining room— that's across the hall—and stripped off some of the ceiling plaster and one of the cross beams had a date on it—1800 the date was. And ——"

"Here you are, ladies," Tony said, and took old-fashioned glasses from a tray for them. "Sorry to have been so long. Adam's rather rushed."

They sipped iced Dubonnet and looked at menus. And heard a deep, pleasant voice saying, "They've really got the Dover sole today."

They looked up from their menus and were smiled down on by a tall, heavy man in, Ann guessed, his sixties. He wore a dark business suit complete (to Ann unexpectedly) with a vest. He bulged slightly under the vest, but he was tall enough to carry a good deal of weight. He had a full face, not quite jowly, and an expression of benignity.

"Oh," Faith said. "Hello, Lawrence. You've had lunch, I take it. This is Mrs. Eric Martin, Lawrence. Mrs. Martin, Lawrence Finch. President of the school board, among other things. Among a good many other things, isn't it, Lawrence?"

"Civic responsibilities," Finch said, and firmed his face for them. But, Ann thought, neither the words nor the firmed face was meant to be taken seriously.

"Since you own half the town," Faith said, but she said it smiling up at the tall, heavy man.

"She always exaggerates, Mrs. Martin," Finch said. "Actually, it doesn't come to more than three eighths." He laughed at that, laughing it off. He said, "I understand you and your husband have rented the Barnes house."

Understanding spread quickly through North Wellwood, Ann thought, and said, "Yes. For the summer."

"Good house," Finch told her. "Not one of the old houses, but a good house. Good solid house. Hope you'll like it there, Mrs. Martin. Like our quiet little community."

Ann was sure they would.

"Don't like to see a house standing empty," Lawrence Finch said. "Glad the Barneses rented it. Didn't know they planned to, actually. We all expected them to come back this spring, as usual. Friends of yours, Mrs. Martin?"

"Lucile and Ralph? Yes. That is, Ralph and my father were very close friends. I've known him and Lucile since I was a little girl."

"Fine people, both of them," Finch said. "Kind of people who belong in North Wellwood. Living in New York now, I understand? Don't see why they'd want to. Have to go in a couple of days a week and can't wait to get back to the country. Well-l-l." The lingered-on "Well" was an omen of departure. He added to it, "Enjoy your lunch."

He started off, but stopped.

"Ought to have everything any day now, Faith," he said. "If you still want to go through with it?"

"Yes, Lawrence. I do want to go through with it."

"Your business, my dear. Give you a ring when it's set."

Faith Powers said that that would be fine and they both watched Lawrence Finch leave the long narrow room.

"Usually," Faith said, "I have the blinis. They make them well here. Creamed chicken rolled in a crepe and browned under the broiler. But if they really have Dover sole—only, probably it would take longer."

They settled on the blinis. Tony approved their order. He was rather obviously unsurprised by it.

"The biggest frog in our small puddle," Faith said. "Town supervisor for years, until it was somebody else's turn. Head of the school board since. I was on the board for a few years. Voted off it last

[38]

time around. Walter Brinkley and I. New-fangled notions, that was what we had. Rather a relief to both of us, actually. Only ——"

She stopped abruptly, and then said, "I'm afraid I rattle on, my dear. Perhaps I always did. Poor Arthur."

There was nothing Ann could do but look interested and wait.

"My husband, my dear," Faith said. "Died five years ago last month. Think I'd have got over missing him, but I haven't."

There is still sparkle in this small white-haired woman, Ann thought. She must be nearly seventy, but there is still sparkle. Then she realized she had thought this because, for a quick moment, the sparkle died out of the smooth, round old face, and the young blue eyes.

"Probably," Faith Powers said, "it's the second Dubonnet. Shall we have another?"

"Not I," Ann said, and was told that she was probably right. Mrs. Powers rattled the ice which remained in her glass, and drained the glass. Then there was silence, and it seemed to Ann a tight silence. She loosened it.

"Mr. Finch seems to have liked the Barneses," she said. "To be sorry they're not living here any more."

"Some are," Faith said. "I am, for one. Lucile and I saw a good deal of each other. I'll miss Lucile. And Ralph too, come to that."

"You said they were eased out."

"No, dear. Squeezed out. After Ralph sold a house on the other side of town to Thomas Peters. It's against New York State law to discriminate in the sale of property because of race, color or religion, you know. It's a law easy to circumvent, I'm afraid. Asking prices jump out of reason, and it's hard, I suspect, to prove that they jump with reason. Definite reason. Peters is the only Negro who's been able to buy around here for as long as I can remember. Oh, except on Clinton Street, of course. No village is too small to have its ghetto. Clinton Street is ours. Accepted and glossed over. And white people righteously join the NAACP. I have myself. Ease of conscience, available in the small economy size."

"People resented Ralph's selling Mr. Peters a house?"

"A good many did. Oh, publicly with the usual explanations.

They themselves were all for complete integration. But one thing had to be faced. It would bring property values down. All very regrettable, but there it was. But you know these things, don't you? Probably better than I do."

"Better?"

"Because of your work, Mrs. Martin. On documentaries. Some of them are very good, nowadays." She smiled suddenly. "Oh," she said, "I've looked you up. You know a man named Stuart Leffing? An executive of some sort with UBN? News division, or whatever it's called?"

"I've worked for him."

"He was an instructor at Dyckman years ago," Faith said. "Left us—I still feel I'm part of Dyckman—for greener pastures. A good deal greener, as it turned out. We've, a little, kept in touch. So when Lucile said you and your husband were renting the house— well, I called Stuart. Because, frankly, I saw this thing the network did on the deep South and stayed for the credits. It was a good thing to do, Mrs. Martin . . . Miss Langley."

"Why, Mrs. Powers? Why look me up?"

From where Faith Powers sat she could look out into the narrow lobby of the Maples Inn. She looked now, instead of answering. She looked for several seconds and there was an intent expression on her round, pink face. Ann could not see what Faith was looking at.

Faith Powers turned back to Ann and said she was sorry. She said, "You asked me something?"

Ann repeated what she had asked this quick little woman, under whose wing she had been taken.

"After I talked to Lucile," Faith said. "She—she and Ralph after they'd talked it over—were worried about you. She wasn't too clear why they should be. She isn't always too clear. I mean explicit, really. Something about, 'with that TV show she wrote and all.' "

"I didn't write it," Ann said. "Did preliminary interviews. What on earth did she mean? Why would they be worried about Eric and me? And what would the documentary have to do with anything?"

"It wasn't very favorable to the Klan," Faith said. "Or the White Citizens' Council. People like dear Lawrence talk about Communist influence. It's all coming back from the past, dear. If it ever went away. Lucile and Ralph got to worrying if you—you and your husband—would be made uncomfortable."

Ann could merely shake her head.

"I know," Faith Powers said. "It's hard to put your finger on. This is—call it a conservative community, my dear. More, just now, than I've ever known it to be. All over the country people are taking sides. In a place like this, it's—call it concentrated. Because, in a way which isn't true in the city, we're squeezed together. Not physically, of course. Except on Clinton Street. Squeezed together mentally. And by mores. By an absolute certainty of what is right. And you can take the word 'right' either way. Moral. Right wing. In the last few years there's been a fairly active John Birch Society unit here. It's held meetings, one of them in the high-school auditorium. I don't, of course, argue they shouldn't hold meetings. Say what they like. And that everybody shouldn't. Which, of course, is another matter. I'm . . . tolerated. I was a teacher most of my life. Teachers are notoriously crackpots. Also, my husband was born here, and his father was born here. My people have been here as long. Even now, with the community drawing up sides, that counts. Newcomers— that's another matter. Here comes our food, finally."

Blinis came. Tony was sorry it had been so long. "He had to make fresh crepes."

"Ralph and Lucile Barnes lived here ten years," Ann said. "Newcomers?"

"Oh, yes," Faith said. "By North Wellwood standards, very new." They ate blinis.

"For Eric and me," Ann said, "it's just a place to live for the summer."

Faith said, "Yes, dear," and went on with food. Ann finished her crisply browned cylinders of thin pancakes which enfolded creamed chicken with an admirable wine-flavored sauce. They ordered coffee, and Tony brought it in a silvery pot.

"You say the Barneses were squeezed out," Ann said, "after they sold a house to a Negro? A very prominent one, incidentally. Known all over the country."

[41]

"Yes," Faith said.

"Made to feel unwelcome? But would that have mattered to them —really?"

"Nobody likes to be shut out," Faith said. "Even from places they don't especially want to go into. But there were little niggling things. Nothing they could put their fingers on, really. Their water pump broke down and the plumber, who'd always been very prompt, somehow couldn't make it for two days. Their telephone started ringing in the middle of the night, and just deep breathing on the phone when they answered it. Arnold's—that's the grocery which delivers—began to send them things they hadn't ordered, and to leave out things they needed. Their mailbox got knocked over several times. A few people they knew didn't recognize them on Main Street. Even when they came here there wasn't a table in this room, or in the new room."

She gestured behind her, toward what apparently was the "new room" beyond the bar corridor.

"They had to eat in the main dining room and nobody likes it as well. Sally puts in there people who drop in off the road. Not that many do. North Wellwood isn't really on the road to anywhere in particular. This inn is—oh, more or less the village pub. And, in a way, a club."

"Trivial things," Ann said. "I shouldn't have thought Ralph was— is—a man to let people push him around."

"Little niggling things," Faith said. "I told you that. Not that having a broken-down water pump is really too trivial."

She sipped coffee and poured another splash into her cup.

"Matter of flushing toilets, among other things," she said, with a countrywoman's explicitness. "As to Ralph, yes, I agree. About anything worth the trouble. Living here wasn't, I suppose. Came not to be. With the children grown. If things were to be abrasive ——"

She did not finish that, but looked up, as Ann looked up, at Sally Lambert, tall and gray-haired and smiling down at them, hoping that they had enjoyed their lunch.

More or less simultaneously, they both said, "Very much." Faith added "Sally" and Ann "Mrs. Lambert."

[42]

Sally Lambert was so glad. She had, Ann thought, rather a stingy voice.

"By the way," Faith said, "the thin dark man who was sitting over there." She indicated "over there" with a movement of her head. "He's a new guest, isn't he. I mean, he went upstairs."

"You probably mean Mr. Pederson," Mrs. Lambert said. "Why, Faith?"

Faith Powers shrugged rounded shoulders.

"Thought for a moment I knew him," she said. "Chance resemblance, evidently. He is staying here?"

"Plans to for most of the summer," Mrs. Lambert said. "Working on a book, I understand. Wants a quiet place. A place where people won't bother him. Who did you think he was, dear?"

"Man I knew years ago," Faith Powers said. "I don't really remember his name. Except that it wasn't Pederson."

"Harry Pederson," Mrs. Lambert said. "Quite well known as an author, people tell me."

To that, Faith shook her head and turned to Ann with raised eyebrows. Ann shook her head.

"Of course," Faith said, "there are new writers all the time. Impossible to keep up with. Well, dear?"

The last was to Ann who said, "Yes, I think so."

Tony, who had been carrying a tray of used dishes, put the tray down and pulled their table out from the wall. Sally Lambert hoped she would see Mrs. Martin again and Ann was sure she would.

"Just follow me," Faith said, in the parking lot. "It's only a few blocks. And the jaybird is easy enough to spot, heaven knows."

Ann took it that the Mercedes was "the jaybird." She followed its spurting progress to a parking lot spread widely around a large supermarket.

IV

ANN DROVE THE station wagon into the garage and realized, as she had not before, that it was a two-car garage in name only. If Eric drove his sports car in beside the wagon, he was going to have to exit from it through the roof. One of the cars was going to have to live out-of-doors. Not that that, during the summer, would matter particularly.

One thing had led to another at the supermarket as Ann trundled a cart through its aisles—found bread and coffee and cans of things on shelves; milk and cream and butter and eggs in a refrigerated dairy bin; frozen foods in open-topped freezer compartments. Things had certainly led on to things, Ann thought, raising the tailgate of the wagon and looking into it. I'm as bad in a supermarket as Eric is in a hardware store. Oranges . . . lemons. Did I remember to get lemons?

She lugged heavy paper bags, cardboard cartons, through the back door of the square white house and into the kitchen. She unpacked and put away—in cupboards, in bins, in the refrigerator, and in the freezer. A frozen TV dinner! What ever had made her pick that up? In a supermarket, one buys things because they are there.

She made three trips between station wagon and kitchen. She discovered that, although she had remembered sugar, she had forgotten salt. When she opened a suitable cupboard to stow four rolls of paper towels she found that there were already three rolls in it. It is a problem to awaken a house. I forgot potatoes, because I almost never eat potatoes. But Eric is a meat-and-potatoes man. It's grown very warm for May. I'm a mess.

It was almost five when, finally, she said a resentful "There!" to an unremembered container of turkey tetrazzini and dropped it into the freezer. She banged the lid on it. She went up to take a shower. When she first turned the shower on, water came from it reluctantly and cold. But then the light in the bathroom dimmed for an instant and something, apparently far away, began to go "*uh*-uh, *uh*-uh." After a few moments the shower head spluttered at her and the water flow increased and was, abruptly, very hot. She regulated it and it became, again, almost cold. It also spurted at her. Again she turned the handle which was supposed to regulate the temperature of this erratic water supply.

It settled, finally, to more or less the temperature she wanted, although it was still inclined to waver between extremes. Something, she thought, probably is wrong with it. The pump which had broken down for the Barneses or —— Soaping, she half remembered what, the Friday evening before, she had half heard. Ralph Barnes explaining something to Eric—something which Eric would understand and take care of, if care needed to be taken. Something about something called a pressure tank? Vaguely that seemed right. A pressure tank, whatever that might be, and—wait a minute—"variable pressure." She certainly had that.

She rinsed soap from a slim body. Now the water rushed from the shower head and was just cool enough for comfort. She turned this way and that way under the rushing water, at once soothed and invigorated by its steady beating on her. And the telephone rang. All of the telephones in the house rang and the house seemed to vibrate with their clattering. Ann Martin made the only adequate response to this jangling, which was "*Damn!*" and stepped out of the tub and groped for a towel. Towels hide in strange bathrooms.

She finally clutched a towel from the rack on which she had hung it and dripped on the bath mat. She dried hurriedly and only partially; wrapped the towel around her and that, also, because of the towel's size, only partially. "I'm *coming*," she told the jangle of telephone bells and went out of the bathroom, high-arched feet leaving pad marks behind her. And she thought, It's Eric. Something's happened to hold him up. Or ——

She found the telephone between twin beds and sat on one of them as she reached for it. She said, "Hello?" and was conscious of the worried strain in her voice.

The voice was a man's, and not Eric's.

"We didn't expect you back," the man said. "We thought things had been made clear enough. How clear do we have to make them?"

"I don't know what you're talking about," Ann said. "Who is this? What ——"

"You know what we're talking about," the man said and then said two words—words which had been shouted at Ann Langley over and over a few months before. "Nigger lover," the words were. And then there was the sharp snap of a telephone slammed into its cradle and, after seconds, the hum of the dial tone.

Ann put her own receiver back and sat on the bed, which was gradually becoming damp under her, and looked at the telephone, which seemed to crouch menacingly in the cradle.

She went back to the bathroom, toweling as she went and feeling, as she went, that she had been struck. Ugly words, an ugly voice, can deliver blows as bruising as those a fist can deliver. Because I worked on a documentary, asking questions which were not supposed to be asked and was jeered at for asking them? (And called worse names than this man called me, but was not hurt by them because I expected them.) Not, then, because I am Mrs. Eric Martin. Because, in screen credits, the name of Ann Langley is in a long list of lesser ——

It came to her abruptly as she pulled a panty girdle over hips which did not need its containment.

He was not, she thought, talking to me at all. He was talking, thought he was talking, to Lucile Barnes. He said, "We didn't expect you back." "Back" was the word which counted. It was to Ralph and Lucile Barnes that things were supposed to have been made clear enough. That the Barneses had rented their house was, Faith Powers had made clear, known all over town. But this man, this man with an angry voice, apparently did not know. Then, not part of the town? Of the town which was "squeezed together mentally"?

Ann pulled stockings up slim legs and cinched them to the panty girdle. (Which was what the panty girdle was really for.) She snapped her bra on. She was halfway into a green cotton dress— green goes well with dark red hair—when the telephone rang again.

She thought for a moment she would not answer it. But then she hurried back to the bedroom, because this time it might be Eric—this time it surely would be Eric. He was going to be later than he had expected. She was to come in the wagon and meet him somewhere. He ——

She sat on the still somewhat damp bed and said, "Hello?" into the receiver and waited, tight, for the voice.

The voice, this time, was that of a woman. It was a light, somehow artificial, voice. "Mrs. Eric Martin?" the woman said. "Long-distance call for Mrs. Eric Martin."

"This is she," Ann said, and got "One minute, please" and then another voice, again a woman's voice. This second woman's voice was deeper. Yet, surely, it was not unlike the other.

"Mrs. Martin?"

"Yes."

"This is a friend, Mrs. Martin," the woman said. "With friendly advice."

She speaks, Ann thought, as if she were reading from something. She said, "Who are you?"

"We don't want your kind meddling here," the woman said, still as if she were reading something written down. "A hint to the wise."

Reading clichés written down, Ann thought, and said, "I don't know what you're talking about. Meddling?"

"You know what I'm talking about, all right," the woman said. "Go somewhere else to pry. You're an outsider. Stay outside. You understand."

"No," Ann said. "Not a word of it. Or who you are or what—what any of this is about. And—wait a minute. You keep saying 'here.' But the operator said this was a long ——"

She stopped, because this mysterious "friend," who seemed to be reading from a script, hung up on her.

The other call had been, in an elusive way, almost frightening. This was no more than baffling, yet it, too, brought uneasiness. We came here for a quiet summer, in a place convenient to Eric's job, Ann thought. What have we walked into? What on earth have we walked into?

She went down to the kitchen—the strange kitchen. She stood

[48]

in the middle of it and looked around and tried to decide what she had come to the kitchen for. That lasted only for a second. To decide what to get for dinner, of course. To get ice out of trays, of course.

One of the things she had got at the supermarket was a steak—a thick shell steak, which was the kind they liked. Because, touring the house on Saturday, they had found a portable grill in the garage and a bag of charcoal briquets leaning against it. And because Eric liked to do steaks over charcoal, and did them well. An expensive steak it had turned out to be. But a steak broiled out-of-doors over charcoal would be—would be a kind of celebration meal, a way of welcoming themselves to their new house.

The idea of welcoming themselves, or of being in any way welcomed, to this square white house seemed infinitely remote. Still, they had to eat; they might as well eat as they chose. If, Ann Martin thought, the grill isn't booby-trapped.

The notion—the entirely absurd notion—broke through the mood of uneasiness, and Ann laughed at herself. She was, she thought, taking this much too seriously. The town, with nothing much else to do, was fussing inside itself. Eric and I, she thought, are not part of that. That will be realized and these little "niggling" things will stop. Meanwhile, we can ignore them. Anonymous telephone calls, and many of them more objectionable than these, are fairly common. They are also often obscene. There had been a period, when she lived alone in the apartment in Manhattan, when her telephone had, for more than a week, rung every morning at three o'clock. When she answered it, there had been only the sound of deeply drawn breath. A detective from the local precinct had been sympathetic; he had told her that the city was full of crackpots; advised her to have her telephone number unlisted.

It appeared that not all crackpots inhabit cities. North Wellwood, so seemingly peaceful in its tree-filled valley, obviously had its share.

Ann went out to the garage, leaving the kitchen door open behind her. It was warm outdoors; the sun was still high on this long day. There was a terrace in the rear of the house, with a table and with chairs. Eric could cook their steak beyond it and, if they liked, they could eat steak on the terrace.

The grill had wheels. She trundled it out to what she thought would be a convenient place and carried the bag of charcoal briquets out to it. She went back to the kitchen and rinsed cocktail glasses and put them in the freezer compartment of the refrigerator. She took from the freezer a package of frozen French fried potatoes. (Tomorrow she would get real potatoes.) "Keep frozen until ready to use," the directions told her, and she put the package back. Peas to go with the steak and French fries? They would do. A salad? She had remembered salad greens. But Eric did not much care for salad. Too soon yet to take the steak out to reach room temperature. Particularly on an afternoon as warm as this. Get out ice and put it in the thermos container. There is shade over part of the terrace from a big tree. An ash tree, I think. Probably Eric will know what kind of tree. It will be tranquil there. "Tranquil" is an odd word to come to mind. It is a word for special occasions. I'll tell Eric about the telephone calls and about Faith Powers and about what she said about the Barneses being "squeezed out." I'll have many things to tell Eric and, unless he got held up and if New Canaan is really half an hour from here, he ——

A car which sounded indignant was coming up the drive. She went to the front door to greet car and husband.

Her thin dark husband snapped himself out of the little car. He had driven with the top down and his dark brown hair was ruffled, although he wore it short. And the expression on his face was somewhat more than ruffled. Something's gone wrong, she thought, and went out onto the porch and down the steps to the driveway. She said, "What is it, darling?"

"Some son of a bitch thinks the end of our driveway is part of the town dump," Eric said, and there was anger in his voice. "I had to ——" But he did not finish that. His expression changed suddenly and entirely and he held out his arms to her. He said, "You look swell," and she walked into his arms.

After a moment, they freed themselves.

[50]

"I'll have to find a shovel," Eric said. "Looks like somebody emptied a trash can."

"Out of a car," Ann said. "People throw the remains of picnics out of cars. Unpleasant people."

"Only," Eric said, "there's a dead rat in this mess. A very dead rat."

They had learned—were beginning to learn—that even unpleasant things are best done together.

Eric carried an empty trash can from the garage and down the drive and Ann carried a shovel.

The mess did not look like the remains of a picnic, and the rat in it was indeed very dead. They dragged the partly filled trash can back up the drive, each pulling on one of its handles and Eric carrying the shovel in his free hand. In the garage they put the cover on the trash can, and put it on very firmly.

Walter Brinkley had half wakened from his afternoon nap when the telephone rang. There was a telephone by his bed and he reached for it sleepily and then drew his hand back because it had stopped ringing. Harry had answered it on the extension in his apartment behind the kitchen. Or in the ktichen. Probably the call was for Harry. NAACP, probably.

Brinkley looked at his watch, which told him it was five thirty-six. Time for a shower and shave and an hour's work on *A Note on American Regional Accents* before, more agreeably, it was time for a cocktail on the terrace with some hours of tedious, and at times painful, revision behind him. He bounced out of bed and was in the process of bouncing toward the bathroom when he heard Harry Washington's feet on the stairs.

Harry knocked and then, through the door, said, "Mrs. Powers is calling, Professor."

Walter Brinkley went to the telephone and said, "Good evening, Faith," into it.

"Are you," Faith Powers said, "tied up for dinner? I mean now. Tonight. I realize it's short notice."

Harry had, Walter dimly remembered, said something about leg of lamb. With what was left as curry in the future. Walter Brinkley

[51]

was fond of curried lamb. Of roast lamb, for that matter; although a leg of lamb, even a small one, was more than two men needed for a ——

"No, Faith," Brinkley said. "Short a man, my dear?"

"Not that, really," Faith said. "Perhaps—call it long a man, Walter. And at the inn. Not at my house. And—we may have to loiter. Start early and stay late."

He told her that she was being mysterious.

"I don't," Faith said, "want to precondition you. But—will you?"

"Of course. I'll pick you up."

"No. Meet me there. At around six-thirty, if you can make it. Because I don't know when he ——" She stopped herself. He waited for a second, but she waited too.

"About six-thirty," Brinkley said. "Shall I call Sally Lambert?"

"No," Faith Powers said. "We won't need to, dear. Not so early. Anyway, I'd rather ——"

Again she did not finish, which was unlike Faith Powers, who usually spoke in sentences. A teacher, even at the university level, is trained to set a good example to the wayward, who often speak merely in a casual sprinkle of words.

Brinkley called down to Harry that he would be eating out and if the lamb was in the oven . . .

"Not yet, Professor," Harry called up to Brinkley. "Since we both like it pink."

In the old days, the pleasant and relaxed days, Walter thought, Harry would have said "likes," not "like." Walter sighed and went to shave and shower.

Faith's unmistakable blue Mercedes was in the parking lot of the Maples Inn when Walter Brinkley swerved in his somewhat elderly MG. In the inn's taproom, Faith had the table which faced the cavernous fireplace. Walter said, " 'Evening, Sally," in the entrance hall and got "Good evening, Professor Brinkley," which was carrying formality rather far. He went into the taproom and sat beside Faith Powers.

Faith had a drink in front of her—scotch on the rocks from its size and color, and from Brinkley's considerable experience of the habits of an old friend. She had only had a sip from the glass, if she had had anything. She held the glass awkwardly and Brinkley looked at her hand and finger. "Slammed the car door on it," Faith said.

Tony came in from the bar with a martini on a tray and a small dish of lemon-peel slices. This was gratifying to Walter Brinkley. It was also, if he decided to think about it, a little embarrassing. He decided not to think about it and raised his glass to Faith and continued it to his lips. Adam had remembered to make the martini from House of Lords gin.

The taproom was empty except for one youngish man at a corner table. The youngish man was reading a book and drinking a beer. The book was fat and flat on the table and Brinkley could not see its title. Brinkley regretted this. When he saw someone reading a book he always wanted to know what the book was.

"A *Thousand Days*, dear," Faith told him. "Schlesinger. We have new neighbors. In the Barnes house. A young couple named Martin. At least, she is young. And very pretty. Does the name Langley mean anything to you?"

Faith usually finished sentences. She also usually stayed on subjects. She's disturbed about something, Walter thought, and said that the name Langley did not mean anything to him and asked if it should.

"Mrs. Martin's professional name," Faith told him. "I suppose her maiden name. Did you see the UBN documentary on the deep South? Mississippi, for the most part."

"TV?"

"Yes, Walter. And UBN is the United Broadcasting Network. The documentary ran an hour and a half and was very interesting, and I doubt whether most of the Southern stations carried it. Actually, as I remember it, there was something of a furor about it in Southern newspapers. References to blackening the name of the Southland. Smirching Southern womanhood, for all I know."

"I don't see much television," Brinkley told her. "Or, I'm afraid, read the newspapers as much as I should. Mrs. Martin's professional name is Langley. What is her profession, dear?"

[53]

Faith Powers told her friend what Ann Martin-Langley's profession was, and that she had received credit on the documentary.

Brinkley raised his white eyebrows, which a little needed trimming. He also shook his head. Faith was, he thought, more oblique than he had ever known her to be.

"Lucile is rather worried about them," Faith Powers said. "About the Martins."

"Lucile worries rather easily," Walter said. "Why is she worried this time?"

Faith drank before she answered. She drank rather deeply for her. She was usually a sipper.

"Walter," she said, "I know you live in that book of yours. More than ever the last year or two. Do you know what's going on in this town of ours? How it's—drawing in on itself? And on its past? On what it thinks are the ideas of its past? And, of course, the country's past."

"It's always been conservative, in its sleepy way," Brinkley said. "If that's what you mean."

"It isn't a sleepy way any more," Faith said. "Did you hear about Thomas Peters? Did you know that Lucile and Ralph Barnes were— call it ostracized here. In the end, ostracized out of town?"

"About Peters, yes. And that he insists it was accidental. Harry told me this morning. And about the Barneses. Yes, I gathered that. But Lucile always has been a worrier. I thought—well, that she had made much out of little. I suppose I did."

"You pull this book over your head. Burrow into it and hide."

"Very well, Faith. The absent-minded professor. And emeritus at that. Perhaps I merely hide in the book."

"It will be a fine book," Faith said. "You've let me see enough of it to make me sure of that. Not that, knowing you for all these years, I wouldn't have been sure, anyway. But—have they bothered you? Since we both ran for the school board and got—what do they say?"

"Clobbered," Brinkley said, back on the familiar ground of words. "Snowed under. Routed. The word 'skunked' isn't used much any more, I believe. The synonyms for 'defeated' are numerous. You asked me—oh, of course. If 'they' had bothered me. Who are *they*, Faith?"

She drank again. This time she merely sipped, which somewhat relieved Walter Brinkley.

"Do you mean the Birchites? I do know they've grown surprisingly strong in the community. They ——" He interrupted himself by laughing, unexpectedly to himself. She waited.

"The Misses Monroe are Birchites," he said. "Elvina and Martha. They invited me to a meeting. Sweet little old things. A bit fuzzy, perhaps. And bewildered. The defeat of Senator Goldwater really shook them. And the income tax. They've never understood the income tax. And the United Nations. But harmless old ladies. Old even to me, Faith. Even to me."

"Did you go to the meeting?"

"I meant to. I'm sure I planned to. But it slipped my mind. There was a question in my mind about the use of phonetic symbols and ——" He broke himself off. He said, "Did you go, Faith?"

"Wasn't invited. No, I don't mean members of the John Birch Society. Or, perhaps some of them. I agree, most of them are harmless. As harmless as 'Monroe, Misses, the.' "

(Elvina and Martha Monroe were so listed in the Brewster telephone directory, of which North Wellwood is an afterthought. The listing had long amused both Walter Brinkley and Faith Powers.)

"Repeal of the income tax," Faith said, and ticked that off with her thumb. "Withdrawal from the United Nations." The index finger of her left hand withdrew the United States from the United Nations. "The Labor Relations Act." Her middle finger did for that. "Reciprocal trade relations" took care of a ring finger which had a wedding ring on it. "Forced integration." She used her little finger for that, and then, unexpectedly to Brinkley, clenched the small, plump hand into a fist. It relaxed almost at once.

"Nostalgia," Brinkley said. "A hopeless yearning for a different time. In a way rather touching. Although I suppose, for some of them, there's money in it. The Misses Monroe contribute, I shouldn't wonder."

"Turning back the clock, in the old phrase," she said. "Not that

[55]

and flowed up from her knees and to the breakfast tray. She took a napkin from it and went back to the cat.

It was not, Merton noticed, the usual breakfast paper napkin. It looked like being a cloth napkin. And Susan had used the silver coffeepot, instead of the crockery pot which was usual for terrace breakfasts.

Special things, Heimrich thought. In celebration of the promotion a week ago. She thinks—has for a long time thought—that my being called "Inspector" instead of "Captain" is going to mean that I keep regular office hours. The dear one. The poor deluded darling. Hoping for a better regulated hippopotamus.

Susan was down on her knees again, and this time the little black cat did not back away, but let Susan rub the napkin gently along his back. Then the little cat, very suddenly, lay down and rolled over so that Susan could dry his belly. "Not a white hair on him anywhere," Susan said. Heimrich, looking down at Colonel's present, had noticed that. "A tomcat," Susan said. Merton Heimrich had also noticed that. "Pretty kitty," Susan said, continuing to dry. She looked at Colonel, who still lay in his collapsed fashion on the terrace flags.

"Where on earth?" Susan asked the big dog.

Colonel turned his head away, resting it on an enormous paw. He went so far as to whimper slightly. He did not look at Susan.

There is not really much point in being a dog. A dog goes to the trouble of bringing a friend home and what is his reward? Humans make a fuss—a rather ridiculous, much too concerned, fuss—over the guest. But do they thank the dog? You'd think, from the way they act, the dog wasn't around at all. Dogs always get the worst of it.

"You're making the monster jealous," Heimrich told Susan.

Colonel does not mind being called "the monster." So far as the Heimrichs have been able to determine he regards it as a term of endearment.

"Is a good dog," Susan said rather absently. "Is a fine dog." She continued to dry the cat. Colonel did not bother even to flap his tail. "He's purring," Susan said. "He's got a big purr for such a little cat."

[62]

Heimrich got up and went to the breakfast tray. He filled two cups, putting cream in his, and cracked his soft-cooked eggs into their cup. He put the cup of black coffee on a flagstone beside Susan, where she could drink it if she had a hand free. He carried his own coffee and eggs to the table by which he had been sitting.

"The mite is starving, probably," Susan said. "Bring the cream while you're up, will you?"

Heimrich was no longer up. He got up and got the cream pitcher and put it down on the terrace beside Susan's coffee cup. In all reason, Heimrich thought, it is impossible to be an object of grace while sitting cross-legged on a flagstone and drying a wet cat. But reason does not enter into such matters. Heimrich watched while Susan took her cup from its saucer and poured cream into the saucer and moved the saucer in front of the little black cat.

"Feed a cat and you've got a cat," Heimrich told her. "It's a rule."

"I know," Susan said. "Laid down by cats. Here, mite."

Mite rolled to four paws and leaned to sniff the cream. He looked up at Susan and made a small sound. "You're very welcome," Susan told the little cat. "Get on with it, mite."

The little black cat got on with it. Susan drank black coffee and Merton spooned his eggs. Colonel whimpered. (Dogs get left out of everything.)

"Probably he belongs to somebody," Susan said, and flowed from terrace flagstone to chair. "Where on earth do you suppose Colonel found him? And how did Colonel know not to hurt him?"

"Where did you find him, Colonel?" Heimrich asked the big dog, who moved an ear in the direction of the familiar voice and let it go at that. "Big dogs sometimes carry things gently," she told Heimrich and considered for a moment and added, "Ducks."

"Ducks have feathers," Susan said. "Anyway, that's retrievers. Not Danes. And ——"

The telephone rang in the house. Colonel reared, in segments, to his feet, looked for a moment at Heimrich, and started toward the house, presumably to answer the telephone.

"Probably," Susan said, "somebody to ask if we've stolen a cat." She started to get up and was told to finish her coffee. Heimrich got up from his chair and followed his dog, feeling that he lumbered—that even by comparison to Colonel he had a lumbering gait. A lumbering old man, Heimrich thought, destined, and properly, to spend the few remaining years of his life behind a desk at Hawthorne Barracks. He also thought it would not be somebody asking about a lost black tomcat, unless, of course, somebody had seen Colonel steal him from somewhere.

Colonel blocked the doorway into the house, as was his custom. Heimrich kneed him out of the way, as was his. The telephone continued to ring. Heimrich reached the telephone and stopped its ringing and said his name into it. He listened and said, "Go ahead, Charlie," to Lieutenant Charles Forniss, also newly promoted, and speaking from Hawthorne Barracks, headquarters of Troop K, New York State Police.

"Locals at the other end of the county think they've got a killing," Forniss said. "Looked like a routine smashup at first. Maybe not routine. Car went over an embankment into a gravel pit and rolled a few times and burned. Along with the driver. Only, hour or so ago they did an autopsy. Bullet in the brain."

"Where, Charlie?"

"Place called North Wellwood," Forniss said. "We've been there before, Inspector. Thought I'd take Ray Crowley along. O.K.?"

"Yes," Heimrich said. "Only ——" He paused for a moment, remembering that he was an inspector and had many things to supervise; remembering that Forniss was a lieutenant now and due to be in charge. He said, "Who's the victim, Charlie?"

"Woman named Faith Powers," Forniss said. "Mrs. Faith Powers. Fairly prominent in the community, from the way the locals talk. All right to get along, M.L.?"

I should, Heimrich thought, go to the office and shuffle papers and put initials on them. I should assign others; delegate authority, as becomes an inspector. It is time authority is delegated to Charlie Forniss, who's a good cop. On the other hand—North Wellwood.

"Get along, Charlie," Heimrich said. "I'll join you there."

He went back to the terrace, after kneeing Colonel out of the way. Susan watched him coming toward her and thought, briefly, how well he carried himself for a man so big—for any man, come to that —and said, "About the cat?" although by then she had seen his face and knew it was not about the cat.

He told her what it was about.

"It's Charlie Forniss's case?"

"Well," Heimrich said, "I do know people there, Susan. People who maybe can help. Professor Brinkley. You remember him."

"Yes," Susan said. "I remember him, Inspector." She stood up and moved toward him and put her hands on both his arms and looked up at him.

"Finish your coffee before you go, firehorse," Susan Heimrich said. She smiled up at him. "Oh," she said, "I knew all along it wouldn't work." . . .

Heimrich did not drive fast from Putnam County down to Westchester, nor across Westchester to North Wellwood, which lies near its northeastern line. It took him almost an hour to cover the forty miles. He found Forniss at the state police substation, which had relayed word from the chief of the—three-man—police force of North Wellwood.

Victim: Mrs. Arthur Powers, widow. Given name, Faith. Age, late sixties. (Precise age not yet established.) Retired Associate Professor of English Literature, Dyckman University. Former member of the school board, Town of Wellwood. Member of the board of directors, Community Center, North Wellwood. Time of death, eleven-thirty the night before or within a few minutes of that time. Cause of death, gunshot wound occipital area of the brain. Bullet recovered, but battered beyond identification. Apparently twenty-two calibre long. Body badly burned. Bandaged right-hand finger. Minor fracture which had been healing. Place of death, a gravel pit below Long Hill Road, which was north of the hamlet of North Wellwood; which branched from Main Street after Main Street had become Brewster Road; which partly circled the village.

"How do you know when it happened?" Heimrich asked the trooper assigned to the North Wellwood substation.

"People named Trowbridge," the trooper told him, and looked at

Lieutenant Forniss, who had already had the question answered and who gave Heimrich the answer.

The people named Trowbridge, who lived about two hundred yards beyond the place the Powers car had broken through a guard rail and plunged into a gravel pit below, were turning out their lights and locking up their house at eleven-thirty, or a few minutes after that. They could fix the time with reasonable certainty. They had watched, on television, a motion picture which ran until eleven. They had watched news for half an hour. Gerald Trowbridge had gone to the front door to close it and lock it for the night when he heard the crash. Within seconds, he had seen fire leaping in the gravel pit. He had called the volunteer fire department and heard its siren begin to summon volunteers as he ran across the road and slid down the steep slope to the fire. He could not get near the car because of the leaping flames.

"Trowbridge didn't hear a shot?" Heimrich asked. "Before he heard the car crash?"

Forniss looked to the trooper.

"Got him on the telephone," the trooper said. "After the autopsy report came through. He says he didn't hear a shot. To notice, anyway. In the country, though, people get so they don't ——"

The telephone interrupted him. "Probably that damn horse loose again," the trooper said. "'Scuse me, sir." He answered the telephone, saying, "Trooper Arthur, state police." Then he said, "Why, yes, Professor," and listened and said, "Anything you can tell us, sir. We certainly ——"

"Hold it a minute, Arthur," Heimrich said. "Professor Brinkley, by any chance?"

Trooper Arthur said, "Just a moment, sir," into the telephone and put a hand over the transmitter and said, "That's who it is, Inspector. He ——"

"Friend of mine," Heimrich said. "About Mrs. Powers's death?" The trooper nodded his head. Heimrich went across the little office and took the telephone from Arthur, who stood up to hand it to him. Heimrich said, "'Morning, Walter. Merton Heimrich."

"Inspector, is it?" Walter Brinkley said. "Congratulations, Merton." There had been, since Heimrich had known him, almost always a rising note in Brinkley's voice. There was none now.

"Shocking thing about Faith Powers," Brinkley said. "I find it hard to believe. Hurting to believe." It seemed to Heimrich that Brinkley's voice shook a little. "A terrible thing."

"Yes," Heimrich said. "She was a friend of yours?"

"For a good many years," Brinkley said. "Here. When we were both at Dyckman. A great many years, Merton. She was a fine person. It's around town it wasn't just an accident. At least, that's what Clay Foster says. He's editor of the local newspaper. Heard I had dinner with Faith last night. At the inn. Seems Sally Lambert—she runs the inn—told him we were there. And that it was unusual."

"Was it?"

"Yes, somewhat. And I don't suppose there's any significance but—" Brinkley let it hang for a moment. Then he said, "Perhaps there's something I ought to tell you about. May be a waste of your time. But in view of this awful thing, I ——" He paused again. "Telephones," Walter Brinkley said, "are, to me, most unsatisfactory substitutes. Shall I come to the substation?"

"You're home now?"

"Yes."

"Wait for me, Walter. I'll be around. And did you tell whatever it is to this Mr. Foster?"

"No. That is, that Faith and I had dinner, of course. At her suggestion. No more than that."

"Then," Heimrich said, "don't. Until you've told me whatever it is."

"Almost certainly not of importance," Brinkley said. "But I did think of that, Merton."

"Ten minutes," Heimrich said.

"O.K.," Brinkley said, a little to Merton Heimrich's surprise. Heimrich had, of course, no knowledge that Brinkley was some paragraphs under the spread of "O.K." throughout the world and was slightly obsessed with its variants, including "oke."

"They haven't hauled the car up yet," Lieutenant Forniss said, after Heimrich had hung up. "Got the road blocked off until we have a look, M.L. If you're going to see Professor Brinkley . . . ?"

"Yes, Charlie," Heimrich said. "You and Ray."

The telephone rang again. Trooper Arthur answered it. He listened. He said, "All right, we'll get on it as soon as we can, sir." He put the receiver back in its cradle.

"Was the horse this time," he said. "Olmstead's horse. Rolling in the Burnsides' garden. Pesky beast. Cliff Burnside's snap beans were just beginning to show." He shook his head. "Cliff *will* plant them early," he said. "If it hadn't been that damn stallion it probably would have been frost. Still . . ."

There were barricades where Long Hill Road diverged from Main Street which, imperceptibly, had become Brewster Road. Crowley got from behind the wheel and cleared a path for the car. They drove uphill on a narrow blacktop for about a quarter of a mile. It was, Forniss realized, a "good" part of North Wellwood. Smooth driveways led from either side of the road and led far back to big houses, screened by trees. An odd place for a gravel pit, Forniss thought.

A uniformed trooper stepped into the middle of the road and held up both hands to stop them. When Crowley stopped the car, the trooper came up to it. The car was identified only by its lengthy whip of radio antenna.

"This road is—" the trooper said, before the length of antenna registered. Then he said, "Good morning, sir," taking no chances. He said, "Just on ahead, beyond the bend."

They got out of the car and walked around the bend with the trooper. A tow truck was parked beside the road and two men sat in it, smoking. One of them said, "It's about time," when the three were abreast of the truck. He added, expectedly, that they didn't have all day to sit there.

There were no skid marks on the road. There was a jagged hole in the low timber fence which served inadequately as a guard rail. Beyond the rail the ground sloped, gradually at first and then precipitously, to the pit which had been dug for gravel. They stood in the fence gap and looked down—down for more than a hundred yards—at what remained of a bright blue Mercedes. Not much remained of it. Of its once gay color nothing remained at all.

Deep furrows led from the gap the car had broken in the guard rail—led down the slope to the cliff bulldozers had created as they chewed gravel out of the slope. The car had plunged over the cliff.

Forniss and Crowley went through the gap and followed the car's tracks down the grade, which was gentle at first. "She didn't brake," Crowley said, his eyes on the furrows. "No," Forniss said. "Dead. Unconscious, anyway."

"Didn't go over headfirst, at a guess," Crowley said, when they were at the brink of the gravel pit. "Hit something and—hit that." He pointed to an outcropping of rock.

The rock was scarred. Bright blue paint was imbedded in the scarred surface. "Fender, probably," Ray Crowley said. "Swerved it around and then it rolled." They could see on the steep side of the pit where the car had rolled. They had to go almost a hundred paces to the right until they came to a place where the slope was gradual enough for them to work their way down to the bottom of the pit. "Have to haul it up about here," Crowley said. "Don't envy them the job."

The car was on battered wheels when they got to it—the blackened metal which had been a gay and leaping car. The volunteer firemen had wrestled it upright when it was cool enough to touch and had got out of it the body of Faith Powers. The body had been badly burned, except for the face. By some chance, as the body tumbled in the tumbling car, the body's face had ended with arms shielding it. Trooper Arthur had told them that. If it hadn't been for that it might have taken them a long time to identify the body of Mrs. Powers.

"Not much to tell us anything," Forniss said. "Won't be that much by the time they drag it up." But he got down on the ground and looked under the front of what had been a Mercedes convertible. The front wheels had been wrenched apart. There was no way for Forniss to tell whether the steering had failed before the

[69]

car plunged. Perhaps technicians could tell after the car had been taken apart—after there had been, in a way, an autopsy on the car.

A truck trail led from the lower level of the pit in a wide circle and then, where the grade permitted, up to Long Hill Road. Trees had been bulldozed out as the pit was dug and pushed to the side and, not very completely, burned. Below the pit there was a brook and beyond that wooded land climbed gently to the next ridge.

"Must have been a pretty little valley before they started digging," Crowley said.

"Yep," Forniss said. "Must have been. Have to have a special permit to do this sort of thing, Ray. Funny the town let them, wouldn't you say?"

They climbed back the way they had come and Forniss told the trooper the tow truck could go ahead with it.

"Happen to know who owns this land?" Forniss asked the trooper. "Who's been digging the pit?"

"Mr. Finch," the trooper said. "Owns most everything that side of the road down to Main Street. Lawrence Finch, that is."

The trooper spoke as if the name should mean something to Forniss. It did not.

"Live around here? This Mr. Finch?"

"Half a mile up the road. Around a couple of bends. Big white house. Used to be one of the Bennington houses. Dates back God knows when."

"Couple of bends," Forniss said. "Probably can't see this hole in the ground from the house, can he?"

"Shouldn't think so, sir."

"He had a permit for the pit, of course?"

"Around here," the trooper said, "Mr. Finch can get a permit for most anything, Lieutenant. Mr. Trowbridge tried to stop it, from what they say. Said it was defacing. Of course, Mr. Trowbridge lives right up there ——" He pointed. "Mr. Trowbridge can see it," the trooper said. "Hear it, too, when they're working."

Crowley drove the police car up the driveway to the Trowbridge house, from which one could certainly see the gravel pit.

Gerald Trowbridge had gone into the city, as he did—his wife said—four times a week. Mrs. Trowbridge, who looked to Forniss like a youngish woman who spent a good deal of time on a golf course, was quite certain about the time they had heard a car crash through the guard rail, then heard the sound of rending metal as it plunged into the pit. "It was awful to hear." The flames had showed almost immediately and leaped high. No, they had not heard the shrieking sound rubber makes on pavement when a car is braked and braked hard. No, they had not heard a shot. "Not to notice." At the latest it had been eleven thirty-five when the car went through the rail.

"She was such a gay little old lady," Mrs. Trowbridge told them. "She drove what she called the jaybird like a bat out of hell."

She went out with them to their car and looked down, beyond the road, at the gravel pit.

"It used to be so pretty," she said. "So soft and—and gentle. I suppose he's making a lot of money out of it. From what we had to pay the last time we had the driveway resurfaced." And then the deeply tanned Mrs. Trowbridge said, quite unexpectedly to both men, "The self-righteous son of a bitch." . . .

"May as well see where she was heading," Forniss said, as they neared the lower end of the Trowbridge's long—and smoothly graveled—drive. Crowley turned the car left on Long Hill Road, and so in the direction Faith Powers had been going when she died.

The road was narrow and full of curves and wound uphill for three miles. On their left, as they curved to the hilltop, there were large houses, all white, all far back from the road. Mailboxes were lettered with the names of the owners of the houses. They slowed a little when they passed a mailbox lettered Lawrence Finch and looked up the driveway it was set beside. Finch's house was just as white as the others, and larger than most.

They went downhill for a little over two miles and the road curved sharply to the right and became South Lane.

They followed South Lane back to the Main Street traffic lights.

recognized the two who, years before, had come publicly to the defense of his right to say what he wanted to say. He had not, so far as Brinkley had noticed, looked at them with any special attention. On the other hand, after their first brief, and insofar as possible shielded, scrutiny they had not looked at the thin dark man, drinking at his table at the end of the room.

"He was there when you left?"

"Yes."

"He came in with—what did you say the man's name is?"

"Finch. Lawrence Finch. He came in at almost the same time. A few seconds later. That's not the same as saying he came in *with* Larry Finch, is it? They did not really seem to be together. Finch went into the bar. Nagle—if it was Nagle—went to the table and had his drinks there."

"About Mr. Finch?"

"One of the community's rich men," Brinkley said. "Prominent in almost everything. Was town supervisor for a couple of terms. He has a brokerage office in the city, I understand. He is also a vice-president of the North Wellwood Savings Bank. Faith thought he's probably a Birchite but that may be merely rumor. He owns a good deal of property, particularly on Long Hill Road."

"A good place to own land?"

"Estate land, they call it," Brinkley said. "Yes, I suppose it is. Although there's been grumbling about that since Ralph Barnes sold a house there to Thomas Peters." He paused there and looked expectantly at Inspector M. L. Heimrich. For a moment, Heimrich felt that he was not living up to expectations. Then it came to him.

"The lawyer?"

"Yes," Brinkley said. "That Peters."

"It was resented?"

"Barnes's sale to him? Yes, Merton. By a good many. Even before the club thing came up."

Heimrich could merely raise eyebrows to that and wait. Brinkley told him about the club. He showed him the anti-club broadsheet. Heimrich said, "Hm-m-m." He put the mimeographed sheet in his pocket.

[74]

"I think," Brinkley said, "that Faith planned to put some money in the club—buy stock or whatever it is. It's a corporation, so I'd assume it's stock."

"She had money?"

"A good deal, I think. She married rather late. Arthur Powers was, by my standards at least, a rich man. He died some years ago and, I suppose, left his money to Faith."

"No children?"

"No. She must have been in her late forties when they married. A spinster. But not, I'd guess, an old maid in anything but a technical sense. She was always a gay person. When she was younger, a very good-looking woman."

"What they call left wing?"

"Good heavens, no, Merton. An old family here, as her husband's was."

Brinkley, who was usually exact in his phrasing, seemed to think that he had answered exactly.

"Is Mr. Finch's one of the old families?"

"You rather jump around, don't you, Merton? No, not in the sense you mean. His father moved here from Connecticut, I think. Or perhaps it was his grandfather. It was his father, I've always understood, who bought a great deal of land when land was relatively cheap. From farmers, probably. It's bad farming land."

"Barnes?"

"What about Barnes? A good neighbor. Very pleasant, intelligent sort of person. So is Lucile. What about them? Because they sold a house to Mr. Peters?"

"I don't know, yet, what about anybody, Walter," Heimrich said. "I suppose I meant, an old family hereabouts?"

Barnes had not been. He and his wife had bought a house—the house he sold to Peters—about twenty years before. They had had young children then—or youngish children. Brinkley understood they had previously lived on Long Island.

"Long Hill Road is tricky in the winter," Brinkley said. "A school bus skidded off it when the Barneses lived there. Nobody hurt, really. But it worried Lucile, who worries a good deal anyway, and they bought the house down this road. Rented the other, off and on. Speaking of Lucile's being a worrier, did I tell you she's worried about this new couple down the road? In the Barnes house?"

"No, Walter. Why?"

Brinkley told Merton Heimrich what Faith Powers had told him about Lucile Barnes's concern for Eric and Ann Martin. It probably, Brinkley said, was an exaggerated concern. He paused for a moment. "I guess it is," he said. "Lucile and Ralph apparently got to feeling they'd let the Martins in for something. Perhaps a repetition of their own unpleasant experiences. They were more or less harassed out of North Wellwood, you know."

Heimrich didn't know. Walter Brinkley told him about the things —the little, niggling things—which had been done to harass the Barneses.

"Trivial things, really," Brinkley said. "Nothing overt, as somebody's shooting Peters was overt."

Walter Brinkley was disturbed today, Heimrich thought. Usually he was direct, succinct. Usually he remembered, very precisely and in order, what he had said or not said.

Heimrich said, "Shooting, Walter?"

"According to Harry," Brinkley said, "Peters thinks it was accidental—a boy with a new rifle. Perhaps that is what he prefers to think, or to say he thinks. And apparently he was only grazed, the second time. Missed entirely the first. Warning shots? As the police call them?"

"Possibly," Heimrich said. "Details, Walter."

Brinkley gave what details he had to give. He said that Harry Washington might know more. But Harry was in town marketing. If Merton wanted to wait?

"I'll see Mr. Peters," Heimrich said. "Let's get back to last night for a moment. You and Mrs. Powers left the inn about when?"

They had left at a little after nine. They had had several drinks— "Faith wanted to talk, drinks went along with it"—and duck flambé for two, which took a little time to prepare. Yes, finished coffee at a little after nine. Yes, he thought Nagle had still been there, then. No—wait. Nagle had finished his dinner. Another man had come

[76]

in; a much younger and bigger man. This younger man had gone into the bar and Nagle had joined him there.

"As if Nagle had been waiting for this other man?"

It could have been that way. It could have been a coincidence. Brinkley was sure, or almost sure, that Nagle and the other man had been standing together at the bar when he and Faith left.

"On the other hand," Brinkley said, "I believe it's quite a sociable bar. Strangers get to talking."

Nothing was very easy to put a finger on. Which, of course, was usual at this stage of any case.

"You and Mrs. Powers," Heimrich said. "You had come in your separate cars. You both live here on Hayride Lane. You were more or less in sight of each other on the way back? Until she turned off at her house?"

"Oh, no," Brinkley said. "Her car was still there when I drove off. You see . . ."

They had gone together out to the parking lot, and Faith had got into her bright blue Mercedes. But then she had said, "What time is it, Walter?" Then it was nine-twenty.

"She didn't wear a watch herself?"

"I was under one of the lights. She wasn't. And the moon was just rising. It was full last night, you know."

"Yes. You told her it was nine-twenty. Then?"

Then . . .

"I have to make a telephone call," Faith Powers said. "I may as well make it here. You go along, Walter. And—thanks for joining me. For helping."

She got out of her car and walked back toward the inn.

"She walked," Brinkley told Heimrich, "with what seemed to me a special kind of determination. Oh, what seems to me now, of course. Hindsight, I suppose. Perspicuity after the fact." He paused and for a second closed his eyes. "When it will do no good," Brinkley said.

He felt now, Walter Brinkley told Heimrich, that, over coffee and just before they left their table, Faith had been debating something with herself. She had been silent for perhaps ten minutes. "Abstracted. As if she were, as we say, turning something over in her mind."

"You think, now, that she finally decided something after she had got into her car? Decided on a course of action which included making a telephone call from the inn, instead of waiting until she got home?"

"It felt like that," Brinkley said. "More exactly, feels like that now."

"The top of her car was down?"

"It almost always was, except in bad weather. It's not really 'down,' Merton. That model has a top which is lifted off."

"From the inn there's more than one way back to Hayride Lane?"

"Several. Country roads lead into one another. The most direct way, of course, is along Main Street to South Lane, with a jog into Hayride."

"The way you took last night?"

"Yes."

"Would one way be by Long Hill Road?"

"Roundabout, but yes."

"It was a pleasant night," Heimrich said. "A pleasant night for a drive, if one felt like driving. And the moon, the full moon, was pretty well up by—say by eleven-thirty."

"It was then?"

"A few minutes later," Heimrich said. "Near enough then, yes."

"There would have been enough light to—to aim by?"

"For a man with good eyes. Eyes he'd given time to adjust to dimmer light. While he waited."

Heimrich stood up. He said, "I'll check things at the—" and stopped, because the telephone rang in the house. For a moment, Brinkley ignored it. Then he started up and said, "I'd forgotten Harry isn't . . ." and bounced into the house, trailing an unfinished sentence behind him.

Heimrich waited. After two or three minutes, Brinkley bounced out again. He looked worried.

"This Mrs. Martin I was talking about," Brinkley said. "Wanted the name of a reliable service station. One with a truck. Some time last night, somebody let the air out of the tires of Mr. Martin's car. Out of all of them. Martin had to take their station wagon to drive to work. Leaves her stranded."

Brinkley looked up for a moment at his tall friend.

"She has a pleasant voice, this Mrs. Martin," Brinkley said. "There was worry in it, of course. She comes from Kentucky, incidentally. But went to school in the East."

Merton Heimrich was familiar with Brinkley's ear for regional origins. Brinkley's recognition of accent had once been very useful. He was tempted to ask what part of Kentucky Mrs. Eric Martin came from, being moderately sure that Brinkley could tell him. He curbed his tendency to wander on bypaths.

"You were able to give her the name of a service station?"

"Reagan's," Brinkley told him. "They're usually very prompt." He paused for a moment. "Used to be, anyway," he added. . . .

Vandalism is not often a concern of Heimrich's, whose concern is primarily with murder. But at the foot of Brinkley's driveway he turned his car to the left, which was away from the village center. Brinkley had told him that that was the way to go and that the Barnes house was about a mile along the road.

Heimrich turned his car up a smoothly graveled drive toward a square white house. The tires crunched on the gravel. In front of the house a not very young sports car sat flatly on the gravel. It looked dispirited.

As Heimrich pulled the unmarked police car in behind the deflated MG, the door of the house opened and a slim young woman with dark red hair came out onto the porch. She wore a yellow, sleeveless pull-over and dark blue slacks and when she saw Heimrich getting out of his car she said, "Oh," in a disappointed voice.

"State police," Heimrich told her. "Cap——" He caught himself. "Inspector Heimrich. You're Mrs. Martin?"

She nodded her head.

"But I didn't . . ." she said, and looked down at him from the porch, puzzlement in her face. A very pleasant face, Heimrich thought it; a rather thin face and a face to look at twice.

[79]

"I was at Professor Brinkley's when you called," Heimrich said. "Did you get hold of this service station?"

"I hope so," she said. "They seemed a little vague. Will send somebody when they can. But it sounded more like *if* they can. Not at first, but after I told them it was the Barnes house."

Little niggling things, Heimrich wondered.

"Also," Ann Martin said, "somebody threw garbage at the foot of the drive yesterday evening and I got two rather strange telephone calls. But we hadn't notified the police. And—you did say 'Inspector'?"

This was with an inflection of surprise, almost incredulity.

Then she said, "There's something else? Eric—my husband?"

Her lips trembled and the words trembled.

"No," Heimrich said. "Nothing about Mr. Martin. About Mrs. Powers. Faith Powers."

Her lips firmed, but she shook her head, this time evidently puzzled. Heimrich had supposed that, by then, everybody in North Wellwood knew.

"What about her?" Ann Martin said. "I've only just met her but she seems so nice. So sweet."

"She's dead, Mrs. Martin. She was killed. Last night."

This was, he was almost certain, news to the slender young woman with dark red hair. From the expression on her face, he thought it bad news to her. She turned and opened the screen door and made a beckoning gesture and he followed her into the house.

"It's hard to believe," Ann Martin said, and said with Heimrich had supposed she would; said what is always said. "She was so alive. Even meeting her once." Ann broke the sentence, ending it with a slowly shaken head.

"When was that?" Heimrich asked her.

She told him of Faith Powers's sudden, friendly appearance the day before; of their lunch at the Maples Inn. She was sitting so that she could look through the open front door and down the drive, and at the limp sports car. There is no great point in talking with somebody who is thinking of something else. Heimrich said, "The tele-

[80]

phone, Mrs. Martin?" and Ann Martin pointed. Heimrich went to it and dialed and got, "State police. Trooper Arthur."

"Know a service station called Reagan's?"

"Yes, Inspector. Mike Reagan's."

"Get on to them, will you? Drive over if you're covered there. About a call a Mrs. Martin made for service. At the Barnes house. Somebody let the air out of her tires. A nuisance to her, naturally. Tell them we'd like them to get somebody over. Tell them as soon as possible. O.K.?"

It was. What an inspector tells a trooper to do always is.

"They'll be along," Heimrich told Ann Martin, and sat where he could see her face. "Mrs. Powers came here to see you. You didn't expect her to?"

"I'd never seen her or heard of her," Ann told him. "But she said Lucile Barnes—Lucile and her husband own this house—had called her up and . . ."

She was a good reporter, Heimrich thought, listening.

"I thought her concern, Lucile's concern, was—oh, I suppose groundless. It wasn't, apparently."

"These two men at the inn," Heimrich said. "Do you know which one she thought she recognized?"

Ann shook her head.

"Was one of them a thin, dark man?"

"Yes."

"Nobody you recognized?"

"No, Inspector."

"This garbage in your driveway? Not merely something thrown from a passing car?"

"When my husband shoveled it up, it half filled one of our trash cans. And—people don't carry dead rats around in their cars, do they?"

"Seems unlikely," Heimrich said. "These telephone calls? Before your husband got home?"

She told him about the telephone calls.

" 'Meddling'? That was the word this woman used? And, not to pry?"

"Yes."

"You felt she knew who you were? But that the man who called first thought you were Mrs. Barnes?"

"Yes. It's confusing, isn't it? Somebody wants to get rid of the Barneses. Think they have come back. And somebody else wants to get rid of the Martins. But what could it have to do with Mrs. Powers's death?"

"Now, Mrs. Martin," Heimrich said. "I don't know that it has anything, naturally. You've no idea what the woman meant when she told you not to pry?"

"No. Unless ——" She broke off, and lines appeared for a moment between eyebrows which were dark, but not as deeply red as her hair.

"I worked on a documentary for UBN," she said. "About conditions in the deep South. It was objective. Or meant to be. It turned out to be difficult to be objective, Inspector. About the Klan. The White Citizens' Councils. We weren't popular."

"Is it generally known, do you know, that you worked on this documentary?"

"There was a long list of names in the credits," she said. "Mine was one of them—my professional name. Langley. I shouldn't have thought many viewers read the names. But Faith Powers apparently did. And at the post office I gave my professional name too, of course, because I get mail under it."

"This club that's being planned," Heimrich said. "There seems to be a bit of fuss about it locally. You know about it?"

"Mrs. Powers told me."

"You hadn't known beforehand. Didn't, let's say, come here—you and your husband—because you'd heard about it?"

"No. Why on earth—oh. You mean to scout out the lay of the land for the network? No, Inspector. Certainly not."

"But such—what do they call it?—reporting in depth. Is that it?"

"A phrase they use. Yes."

"Might be possible?"

Again thought crinkles appeared between her blue eyes. And Heimrich closed his own blue eyes while he waited for an answer.

[82]

"They might think so," Ann said, and spoke thoughtfully. "The affiliated stations in the South might like it, I suppose. I hadn't thought of it. Not really."

But are thinking of it now, Heimrich thought.

"Your husband," Heimrich said. "Is he connected with UBN too?"

"Good heavens, no," Ann said. "He's an electrical engineer. Designs devices. Things I don't understand at all. He's associated with a firm called Hurst Electronics, and they're doing work for the Navy. They have a laboratory—factory, whatever it is—in New Canaan. That's why we came here. So Eric could drive to work."

"For the Navy," Heimrich said. "Secret devices?"

"'Restricted' is the word they use," Ann Martin said. "Yes. At least, Eric had to be cleared. Navy Intelligence was all over the place for a while, he said. That was before we met."

Heimrich said he saw. He said, "Did you ever hear of a man named Nagle, Mrs. Martin? Aaron Nagle?"

"Patriots United? Yes. Oh, yes indeed, Inspector. They were supposed to be around in Mississippi when we were working there. Nagle himself—he's the head of them, apparently—was supposed to be around. We tried to find him, but most of the people wouldn't admit they'd ever heard of him. Or of this Patriots United. We felt —I felt, anyway—that some of them were afraid of Patriots United and that some of them were covering up for it. They cover up a lot of things—who's a Klan member, except for the spokesmen, of course. Oh, they let us film part of a Klan meeting. A rigged part, we thought. Not as well rigged as they thought it was, actually."

"You were objective, naturally?"

"Oh," she said, "entirely. Stuart—Stuart Leffing—wouldn't have it any other way. He produced it, you know. And he's a very scrupulous man, Inspector."

"About this Patriots United. A right-wing organization of some sort? According to what you people heard?"

"A kind of underground, I think," she said. "A terrorist organization. Their spokesmen—Nagle isn't one of them, so far as I know— admit they're caching arms. For guerrilla warfare against the Communist take-over."

[83]

"You never were able to prove that they had—call it a gang—in Mississippi when you were making this documentary?"

"No. We had—the crew had—a couple of cameras smashed. The local police, the local sheriffs, were very concerned. Said it must be somebody from outside. And Jimmy Powers—he was one of the interviewers—got beaten up. Outsiders, again. Communist agitators, probably. Or what they call 'nigras' when they're being polite in the presence of the Northern press."

"By the way, Mrs. Martin," Heimrich said, "were you born in Kentucky?"

"Louisville. But what on earth?"

"Nothing," Heimrich said. "Oh, curiosity. Professor Brinkley said he thought you were. And educated in the East."

"Smith," Ann Martin said. "From just listening to me on the telephone?"

"He's writing a book on regional accents," Heimrich told her. "Quite an ear for them. Placed me for western New York within fifteen minutes of the time we first met. Have you any idea when the air was let out of the tires?"

She had not. She supposed after dark, but that was merely guessing. It could have been almost any time after Eric left the car in front of the house. After, that was, they had shoveled up the refuse in the driveway.

They had lugged the half-filled can into the garage. Then Eric Martin had started a charcoal fire in the grill. "That's at the rear of the house," Ann said. "By the terrace." Then he had gone upstairs to shower and shave. Ann herself had spent that time in the kitchen, making a list of things she had put into the freezer; reading directions for the preparation of frozen French fries and of broccoli spears, also frozen. When Eric had changed he had made them drinks and they had sat on the terrace. After drinks, he had broiled the steak and she had put the potatoes in the oven, according to directions, and the frozen broccoli in what seemed to her an insufficient quantity of water, although the instructions were firm. The broccoli charred a little.

They had eaten on the terrace. They had put dishes in the dishwasher and taken coffee and cognac to the terrace and sat there again as it grew dark and then, as the moon rose, light again. They had talked. "I had a great deal to tell him. He had been upset about the telephone calls and at first excited and enraged. He's often keyed up at the end of the day, even of an ordinary day." But as they sat and sipped in moonlight they had both grown relaxed. "He said that we're no part of whatever is going on here in the village and that people will understand that in time. He said we'd probably inherited harassment from the Barneses and if it got too bad we'd do something about it. We both came to think that it wouldn't."

They had gone up to bed at, she thought, about eleven. They had not at any time gone to the front of the house and looked out at the sports car sitting in the moonlight.

"You'd have heard a car drive up?"

She thought so, but could not be sure. "Would somebody have taken the chance of driving up openly?"

"Probably not," Heimrich said. "Probably left a car at the foot of the drive and walked up, staying in the shadows of trees where he could. Mr. Martin didn't plan to put his car in the garage?"

"It's supposed to be a two-car garage," she said. "It isn't, really. At least, I think it isn't. We planned to find out this morning."

They had not been able to, with the sports car squashed on the drive, all resilience flattened out of it. Eric Martin, who had an early consultation at the Hurst plant, had taken the station wagon. "After a good deal of swearing. He doesn't like it at best and we hadn't got around to unpacking it entirely."

"This refuse from the driveway. It's in one of the cans in—I suppose in the garage?"

"All but the rat. Eric buried the rat. It apparently had been dead for some time. Why? It's just old wrapping papers, garbage. One or two bottles. Would it possibly tell you anything?"

"Now, Mrs. Martin," Heimrich said. "We'll look, naturally." He thought with sympathy of Ray Crowley, who would sort, if sorting was to be done. "Conceivably," Heimrich said, "there might be a mailing address on the wrapping paper."

"Is it really worth the trouble? The messy trouble?"

[85]

"Probably not. A good many things turn out not to be, in my trade. But we never know until we look."

"I'll show you where it is," Ann Martin said, and got up and went toward the rear of the living room before Merton Heimrich had a chance to assure her that he could find trash cans by himself. He followed her to a garage, which was certainly going to be a tight squeeze for two cars, and she indicated three covered trash cans. Heimrich took the covers off.

All three cans were empty.

She looked into them blankly, and then up at Heimrich.

"I don't—" she said, and stopped, and then said, "I thought it was some sort of dream. I went right back to sleep, if it wasn't a dream." She looked again at the empty cans. "Which," she said, "it clearly wasn't, was it? Our bedroom is on the other side of the house."

He waited for clarification.

Sometime in the early morning she had dreamed or awakened and thought the sound of a car had wakened her. It was light, she thought. "But when I've been driving for any distance I often dream afterward of cars—of trucks." She had listened, awake or in a dream, and not heard the car, or truck, again. In the other bed, Eric had slept quietly. "He sleeps much more lightly than I do. I thought that if there had really been a noise it would have waked him up. So I decided it was just a dream, and went back to sleep. If I had been awake at all."

"Apparently it wasn't a dream. Had you arranged to have refuse collected? One has to, in the country."

She had not. She did not think her husband had.

"But perhaps Ralph Barnes arranged it for us. He did arrange to have a man cut the grass. Should I call and ask him?"

Heimrich thought it would be interesting to know. They went back to the house and she dialed. Lucile Barnes was in the apartment. Her husband was not. Lucile said, "Are you all right, dear?" and it took a little time—conversations often took time with Lucile Barnes—to explain that they were all right. They were, but something terrible had happened.

Lucile Barnes couldn't believe it. Not *Faith*. It took a good deal of time. Ann circled to the point.

So far as Lucile knew, there had been no arrangement made to collect refuse. Of course, Ralph might have arranged it. When he came back—but that might not be until evening. The place to call was the Bennington Refuse Service. They would come around once a week with their truck and they had always been reliable. Well, reasonably reliable. "The last few months there we couldn't really rely on anybody."

The telephone listed for the Bennington Refuse Service was answered by, from the voice, a rather small girl. Papa wasn't there. He was out on the truck. Yes, she would tell papa when he came back that Mrs. Martin had called. Good-bye, now.

"Why would anybody," Ann asked, "dump garbage and then come back and pick it up?"

"If somebody did," Heimrich said. "That's still only a guess, Mrs. Martin. Perhaps second thought—the thought that the source of the garbage might be identified. Perhaps because circumstances had changed. We'll ——"

They were in the living room of the square white house, the front door open. There was no doubt this time that what they heard was a truck. It was a tow truck and the name of Michael Reagan was on it. A man with REAGAN SERVICE lettered on the back of his coveralls hauled an air hose out of the back of the truck and began to inflate tires.

"If I were you," Heimrich said, "I'd run it into the garage when they've finished. And lock the garage, if it's got a lock."

Ann stood on the porch and watched the police car circle the truck and reviving MG. She watched Reagan Service wind air hose back into the truck. She went into the house to get her purse. But when she returned, the truck had gone. Apparently she had, involuntarily, opened a charge account with Reagan's Service.

She put the MG in the garage and found that the garage had no discernible lock. She pulled the overhead door down and went back to the house and called Hurst Electronics and, after no more than reasonable delay, got Eric and told him that the car was on its feet again and that the nice Mrs. Powers she had told him about was dead. To which Eric Martin said, "My God! What kind of place have we got ourselves into?"

There was no ready answer to that.

"I don't like the idea of your being there alone."

There was an answer to that. It was, "Nonsense, darling. I'll be fine." But Ann detected a lack of conviction in her own voice.

She sat for several minutes by the telephone and looked at nothing in particular, which was the wall opposite. Then she spun the dial again; spun it for eleven digits.

"United Broadcasting Network. Good morning. May I help you?"

"Mr. Leffing, please," Ann told the institutional ear which was associated with the institutional voice.

VII

THE FIRST NATIONAL Bank of Wellwood could not, without a court order so instructing, divulge details of a depositor's account, whether the depositor were alive or dead. The lieutenant should be aware of that.

"She had an account here?" Forniss asked the somewhat portly vice-president to whose desk enquiry had led him.

The vice-president made a steeple of his hands and looked over it for some seconds. Then he said, "May I see your credentials again, Lieutenant Forniss?" He saw them again and looked at them carefully again. He handed them back.

"Yes," he said. "Mrs. Powers had a checking account with us. A sub——" He stopped himself abruptly.

"Substantial," Forniss finished for him. "Thank you. A safe deposit box?"

"Not with us. Possibly with Wellwood Savings."

"Do you happen to know the name of her lawyer?"

The vice-president considered that, over tented finger tips. He was, Forniss thought, wary even for a vice-president.

"Probably," the vice-president said, "Sam Bennington."

Forniss looked at the nameplate on the desk and said, "Thank you, Mr. Bennington," to "R. A. Bennington, Vice-President."

There was a telephone booth in the bank lobby. Lieutenant Forniss dialed and got, "State police, Trooper Arthur."

Inspector Heimrich had called in. He was on his way to see Thomas Peters, on Long Hill Road. He didn't know how long he would be. Probably not long. He was going to the Maples Inn after that. Lieutenant Forniss might meet him there. If it was around lunchtime, they might have lunch there. O.K.?

"Yep. Did you round up the horse?"

"Gone to roll in somebody else's garden, I guess. It's sure a pesky beast."

"Somebody else will call for help," Forniss said.

"You're too damned right," Trooper Arthur said, with marked, if nonregulation, resignation in his voice. The New York State Police have many and varied chores.

Heimrich drove the long way round to reach Thomas Peters's house, taking the route suggested by Trooper Arthur. After about a quarter of a mile on Long Hill Road he was stopped by a tow truck which was lumbering onto it. The tow truck dragged after it what remained of a bright blue sports car. Not much remained of it. Blackened and battered, it dangled behind the truck. The truck and its salvage ground down toward Main Street.

A little beyond where he had been stopped, Heimrich slowed again and looked at the jagged gap a blue sports car, almost certainly with a dead woman at the wheel, had made in an inadequate wooden guard rail. He went on up Long Hill, reading the names on mailboxes. Trowbridge just above the gravel pit. Lawrence Finch somewhat farther along the road. Big houses, both of them. Bennington. Another Bennington, this one "R. A." Neither, Heimrich supposed, proprietor of the Bennington Refuse Service. In old communities names recur, branch from an ancient stem.

The road wound up. Then it began to wind down. The houses were on the left as Heimrich drove toward the south. People who lived in them could look down across Long Hill Road into a pleasant valley with, almost certainly, a stream trickling through it. Except, of course, for the Trowbridges, who could look down into a gravel pit.

A Negro with close-cut gray hair, wearing shorts and a white sports shirt, was riding a three-reel lawn mower over a large spread of lawn as Heimrich drove up a smooth drive toward a big white house. The grass looked in fine shape, Heimrich thought. His own, although revived by the recent rains, still showed brown spots. This one did not. Fertilizer. Probably lime. This was acid soil. Certainly water. Probably from more than one well.

The mower swerved his machine—a new one, Heimrich thought—toward the drive and cut the motor.

The man had a thin face and deep-set eyes. He sat tall on the mower's seat—tall and square-shouldered; even sitting on the mower he looked like a lithe man.

Heimrich stopped his car opposite the mower. Heimrich took a chance. He said, "Mr. Peters?" A good many countrymen mow their own lawns.

The man said Yes, and slid off the seat. He was even taller, standing, than he had looked on the mower. He walked a few long steps toward Heimrich. He was medium brown. For an instant he reminded Heimrich of somebody whose picture he had seen in, he thought, the New York *Times*. A young man who, tennis racquet high, body perfect in symmetry, had looked like a statue. Of course. Arthur Ashe. This man was years older; perhaps thirty years older.

"State police," Heimrich said. "Your grass is in fine shape, Mr. Peters. Lime it this spring?"

Thomas Peters had a wide, rather thin-lipped mouth. It widened further into a grin.

"Yes," Peters said. "Nice of the state police to take an interest."

Then the grin disappeared, but a faint smile remained.

"However," Peters said, "I assume there is something else?"

"One or two things," Heimrich said. "Ride you up to your house, Mr. Peters? My name is Heimrich, by the way. Cap—Inspector Heimrich."

"Brass," Peters said pleasantly, and got into the car. "Flattered, Inspector. A little puzzled, of course. Since I didn't make a complaint. I'm assuming it is about somebody's nicking me?"

"Among other things," Heimrich said, and stopped the car in front of the large white house and followed Peters into it. They walked into a square entrance hall, white-paneled, with, unexpectedly, a fireplace at the far end. There were doorways on either side, and a slim young woman came through one of them. Her skin was, by several shades, lighter than Peters's. Her brown eyes were very large. At a guess, she was younger than Peters by at least twenty years. She was also beautiful.

[91]

"Inspector Heimrich of the state police, dear," Peters said to her. "This is my wife Marian, Inspector. Her parents named her after a great singer of our race."

"A very great singer," Heimrich said. "Good morning, Mrs. Peters."

"We should have reported it, Tom," Marian Peters said. "I told you we should have. A gunshot wound, however trivial."

"That applies to the medical profession, my dear," Peters told her. "Right, Inspector?"

"We like to be told," Heimrich said. "But, yes. Reports required from doctors. I gather you didn't go to one, Mr. Peters?"

"It's a scratch," Peters said, and tapped his right shoulder. "My wife used to be a nurse, Inspector. She put an adhesive bandage on it."

It was interesting, Heimrich thought, that both of them assumed that the "nicking" was the reason for his visit. By now news of Faith Powers's murder must be all over. Such news soaks through a small community within hours. Mrs. Powers had died only a little way down the road Thomas and Marian Peters lived on. Peters was a lawyer. It was odd, perhaps, that he should attribute the visit of a police inspector to so trivial a matter.

"Come in here," Peters said, and moved toward the doorway on the right of the entrance hall. Standing in it he turned and again a grin widened his wide, thin-lipped mouth. "And you, Marian," he said, "stay off that mower. It's too big for you."

Marian Peters said, "Yah to you." She went back through the other doorway. "Loves the thing," Peters said, and walked toward two chairs near an open window. "Have a time keeping her off it, now that Mike O'Connor has had to curtail his operations."

There was, Heimrich thought, an inflection of quotation marks around the word "curtail."

"Mike O'Connor?" Heimrich said. There was no special reason to hurry to the point, whatever the point might turn out to be. Air fragrant of lilacs came through the open window—of lilacs and of grass new-cut.

"O'Connor Landscaping Corp.," Peters said. "Sends gangs around to cut grass. Did until a couple of weeks ago, anyway. Plows driveways in the winter. Seems he's taken on more than he can handle. Inconvenient. On the other hand, I rather enjoy riding the mower. How did you happen to hear about somebody's accidental shooting at me, Inspector?"

"Mr. Brinkley told me," Heimrich said. "Got it from his houseman, apparently."

"Professor Brinkley," Peters said, not by way of correction. "Friend of yours?"

"Yes. I've known him several years."

"Since the Wilkins murder, isn't it?" Peters said.

"Yes."

"I thought I remembered your name from somewhere. Isn't an accidental shooting a little out of your line, Inspector? Somebody gives a kid a new rifle for his birthday. He goes out and shoots it."

Peters shrugged his square shoulders. But then he touched his right shoulder tenderly.

"You really think that's the way it was, Mr. Peters?"

"Simplest explanation."

"The most likely?"

With that, Heimrich closed his blue eyes, and waited. He has a theory, which he does not himself try to defend, that he can hear more clearly with his eyes closed; hear the inflections of a voice free from the expressions on a face. Now, for some seconds, he heard nothing at all. He could feel that he was being looked at intently. He opened his eyes. He was being looked at intently.

"If not," Peters said, and spoke slowly. "If not, noticeably bad shooting. Or careful shooting. You can take your choice."

"Careful?"

"With intent to warn," Peters said. "Not to injure or kill. It's that you're after, isn't it, Inspector?"

"Part of it," Heimrich said. "Tell me what happened." He paused for a moment. "Both times," he said.

"I gather," Peters said, "that Harry's been a thorough reporter. Harry Washington's a friend of mine, Inspector. And he's upset. He and Brinkley are oddly close, I think. In spite of the difference in their status." He paused again. "And the color of their skins," he added. "Yes, there were two shootings. It was this way . . ."

The first shooting had been ten days or so before. Peters had driven up from his office in the city, and got home rather late. It was already beginning to get dark. He had run his car into the garage and, from it, turned on the light which illuminated the driveway. He had stepped out and heard the sound of a shot and then, almost at the same instant, the sound of something hitting a tree.

"Half a dozen feet from where I was," Peters said. "I recognized the plunk. The next day I found a hole in the tree and dug the bullet out of it. A twenty-two."

"You kept the bullet?"

"Yes," Peters said. "I'm afraid I gouged it getting it out. It was in deep. You want it anyway?"

Heimrich did. Peters got up and went to a desk and pulled a drawer open and came back with a twenty-two slug. It was gouged. It was still possible that a comparison microscope might do something with it, if they got that far. Heimrich put the bullet in his pocket.

"You say it was deep in the tree," Heimrich said. "Fired from close by, then?"

"I'd think so."

"The second time? When you were hit?"

The circumstances had been almost identical, but this time the marksmanship had been better. Again, Peters had heard a shot. But this time, again in almost the same instant, he had felt stinging pain in his shoulder. And this time he had dropped to the ground and lain for a moment on the harsh gravel. There had been no second shot.

"Whoever it was may have thought he'd finished you."

"I didn't lie there long," Peters said. "If he'd waited he would have seen me get up. Taken another potshot, if he meant to kill me. No, I think that both times he meant to warn."

"Warn of what, Mr. Peters?"

"That we're not welcome here. We never have been, I suppose. But we've not really been bothered."

"Happen to know," Heimrich said, "whether this man O'Connor is still mowing other lawns around here?"

"I thought you wouldn't miss that," Peters said, and again he grinned at Heimrich. Then he nodded his head.

"I've seen his crew at the Benningtons'. At both Benningtons'. And Finch's place seems well mowed when I drive by it on my way to Brewster."

"This sort of thing has happened only recently?"

"Yes."

"Since your group applied for the club permit? For nonconforming use of a residentially zoned area?"

"Yes. Oh—there's racial prejudice here, as there is everywhere. Not overt, for the most part. Marian isn't invited to join the garden club. Didn't expect to be, or want to be. I'm not one of the local Lions. Don't want to be. But a good many people have been pleasant, Inspector. Gone out of their way to be, which is a kind of thing Negroes have to get used to. Faith Powers, last winter, gave a cocktail party. More or less for us. A good many came. And were cordial as all hell."

For the first time there was an edge of bitterness in Peters's voice.

"Your friend Brinkley was at the party," Peters said. "And the Congregational minister and his wife. Quite a few of the best people."

"Brinkley," Heimrich said, "was he one of the overcordial ones?"

Once again Peters's mouth widened and this time he shook his head.

"Not the professor," Peters said. "I suspect he's color-blind. He did say I was born in New York City and went to school there. Said that was the way I sounded. Quite right, too. Harlem. New York University. Dyckman University Law School."

"Mrs. Powers," Heimrich said. "She wasn't, I gather, one of those who, as you say, went out of their way to be cordial."

"Not Faith," Peters said, and spoke with emphasis. "She's as color-blind as your professor. She's ——"

He stopped because Merton Heimrich was slowly moving his head

[95]

from side to side. An expression of concentration and then concern came over Thomas Peters's lean, dark face.

"I'm sorry," Heimrich said. "I had supposed it would be all over town, Mr. Peters. Faith Powers was killed last night. Shot to death in her car. Just down the road a ways. You hadn't heard?"

Peters shook his head slowly. He said, "My *God*," and then, in an unbelieving voice, "Faith Powers!" and then, again, "My God, Inspector. She was such a shining woman."

For an instant he pressed the palms of his dark hands against his dark forehead. He took them down.

"No," he said, "we hadn't heard. The grapevine stops short of the Peters house, Inspector. Down the road, you say? When, Inspector?"

"Her car ended up in the gravel pit," Heimrich told him. "About eleven-thirty."

And he told the tall lean man the rest of it.

"Not on her direct route home from the inn," Peters said. "And a considerable lapse of time. She did drive around a good deal. Just to drive around. She was very fond of that bright car of hers. And last night was a pleasant night."

"Yes," Heimrich said. "Bright moonlight, Mr. Peters. She wasn't coming here, by any chance?"

"Here? Why should she? The answer is No. At least—I can't be categorical about that, can I? She wasn't expected here. I know of no reason why she should be coming here. She'd have found us asleep if she had. We went to bed about eleven."

I get answers to questions I haven't asked, Heimrich thought. An alert man. And, of course, a lawyer.

"I understand," Heimrich said, "that Mrs. Powers planned to purchase stock in this club you're organizing."

"Do you? What gave you this understanding, Inspector? Not that there's any secret about it, of course."

"Brinkley said he had that impression. I assume he got it from her."

"It's a corporation," Peters said. "Issues stock under New York State law. We've sold a good deal of stock, Inspector. To whites and Negroes. To get the Craig house in condition to serve as a club-

[96]

house. To turn a hundred and fifty or so acres into a golf course. This will cost a good deal of money. The architect estimates a hundred thousand, but I suspect it will run to more. The land itself isn't cheap. No land around here is."

"Mrs. Powers had invested?"

"Taken an option on twenty thousand dollars' worth of stock. The actual sale hadn't been made. She had to convert some securities before she gave us a check, I understand. Most people would, of course. Even people as well off as I assume she was. If what you're getting at is, was she coming here in connection with her investment, I doubt it very much."

"There's opposition to this club, I take it."

"A great deal. We'd expected that."

"Mr. Peters, is the establishment of this country club a—call it a test case?"

"That isn't the intention, Inspector. The intention is to build a pleasant club where people of your race and mine can play golf and tennis, and have drinks and eat. A good many of us like to play golf. Does that surprise you? Some of us have enough money to belong to clubs. And, for a good many of us, objection to segregation cuts both ways. But, if it's what you call a test case, that's not of our making."

His voice had hardened somewhat, Heimrich—who had listened with closed eyes—thought. He clipped his words. Possibly, Heimrich thought, he is trying to convince himself as he convinces me.

"All right," Peters said, although Heimrich had said nothing. "To some of us there may be in it an element of crusade. I don't deny that, and you wouldn't believe me if I did, would you? If it is a crusade, it is one of peace. We need peace just now. Don't you agree?"

"Yes," Heimrich said. "How did you happen to pick this community, Mr. Peters?"

"Suitable land with a suitable big house on it. A landowner who is anxious to sell what to him's a white elephant. There's a limited market for white elephants, Inspector. The Craig house—it was built for another way of life."

"I know the house," Heimrich said. "The bullet that grazed you. You haven't got it?"

"It kept on going," Peters said. "I didn't look for it. It would, I think, have landed in tall grass—meadow grass O'Connor rough-mows twice a year. Or used to. Worse than a needle in a haystack."

"Yes," Heimrich said. "Do you know, or know of, a man named Nagle, Mr. Peters? Aaron Nagle?"

"What the . . ." Peters said, and his eyebrows wrinkled up into his forehead. For once, Heimrich thought, this astute man isn't ahead of me.

"I know of Nagle," Peters said. "He's one of the leaders of, perhaps *the* leader of, something called Patriots United. An organization of right-wing hoodlums. Out west somewhere they drill, with real guns, getting ready to defend the country against Communists. A lunatic fringe."

Unexpectedly, he grinned again.

"Lunacy," he said, "is not a racial characteristic. Neither is hood-lumism. Why on earth do you ask about Nagle, Inspector? He's somewhere out in the West organizing red-necks. And, at a safe guess, getting dues from them. Selling them uniforms and rifles, for all I know."

"Probably he is," Heimrich said. "You're in the civil rights movement, I understand. I thought you might have heard of him."

"An unresponsive answer if I ever heard one," Peters said. "However —— Yes, I'm in the civil rights movement. As a lawyer. Yes, I've told you what I've heard of Nagle and his little gang of hoodlums. And if you mean, would he consider the North Wellwood Country Club, as proposed, part of a Communist front—yes, I suppose he would. But I doubt if he's got a rifle which would shoot from—oh, Arkansas, I think it is—to my garage. Or to this place down the road where Faith was shot. Because she was going to invest in an interracial country club?"

"Now, Mr. Peters," Heimrich said. "So do I, naturally. Do you expect the club's permit to go through?"

"I hope it does."

[98]

Heimrich stood up and, rather obviously, waited for that answer to be amplified. It was not.

Peters stood up. He said, "I haven't helped you much, have I? Not because I don't want to, Inspector."

"I'm sure of that," Heimrich said. "Sorry I had to interrupt your mowing, Mr. Peters. You've got a fine stand of grass."

They walked together, two tall men, out of the living room and through the entrance hall and out of the house.

The power mower was not where Peters had left it. It was far down the wide lawn, nearly at the road. It was being ridden by Marian Peters and it seemed to be moving rapidly. Peters said, "Damn!" and began to run across the grass toward the mower. The mower made a jaunty turn.

VIII

HEIMRICH DROVE FROM Peters's big white house toward the center of the village of North Wellwood. He did not hurry. When he passed the gravel pit he slowed again and looked down into it. It told him nothing, except that today it was not being worked. As a mark of respect for the dead? Or because there were, at the moment, no orders for gravel? It did not matter.

It was, of course, hard to decide what did matter. There was as yet no pattern. Heimrich, as he drove, tried to make a pattern in his mind; tried to bring some shape to things, although he knew it was too early for a shape to form. Still —— It's lumpy, Heimrich thought; lumpier even than usual at this stage. There is no coherence. It is as if, in this small and outwardly peaceful place, a number of things were going on at once, obscurely related and similarly hostile.

He turned into Main Street.

But not, he thought, hostile to the same degree. That was the major "lump." Hostile, presumably, to the interracial country club. Hostile, but that for a long time, to the ownership by Thomas Peters of a large white house in a "good" part of town. This last flaring up now because the club project had brought things to a head? That was probable. But a discrepancy, and a glaring one, remained. As he turned from Main Street toward the North Wellwood substation of the New York State Police, Heimrich had become sharply conscious of the shape of the discrepancy. That was something, if not much.

Somebody had dumped garbage at the foot of the Martins' driveway and had left the air out of the Martins' tires. Small, annoying things. The kind of small annoying things which had happened to the Barneses when they lived in the square white house on Hayride Lane. Such things had the feel of adolescent hoodlumism; of a childish activation of what was perhaps a community's mood. But it had been hoodlumism within limits. Air had been let out of tires by pressing down valve plungers. Not by slashing through rubber. The difference between what was not much more than an unpleasant Halloween prank and vandalism.

But a woman had been shot in the head, almost certainly by an expert marksman, as she drove an open car in the moonlight along a quiet road. And a man had been shot at twice and missed once—by intention?—and very slightly injured the second time. By an inexpert marksman? Or by one very expert indeed?

In neither case, Heimrich was strongly inclined to think as he turned in at the substation, by the same person, or of course persons, who would dump garbage on a drive. Even garbage containing a dead rat.

There was also, he thought as he walked into the substation and tossed up a hand in answer to Trooper Arthur's correct salute— there was also the question of the two telephone calls received by Ann Martin. They had not, evidently, been made by the same person, since one caller thought that Ann was Lucile Barnes returned, and the other knew she was not—knew not only that she was Ann Martin but also that she was Ann Langley, an interviewer for UBN. The second caller had, at a guess, assumed that, as Ann Langley, Mrs. Martin was scouting a story for the network. As Ann Martin said she was not.

Two individuals, or two groups, with similar aims but no cohesion in their methods? Perhaps that was the lump.

Heimrich sat at Trooper Arthur's desk and called the Barracks. He wanted all Barracks could find out about a man named Aaron Nagle, who might sometimes use the name of Henry Pederson. Anything Barracks could find in files or get from the New York City police or, for that matter, from the FBI. Wanted anywhere for anything? Fingerprints on file anywhere? Barracks would know what to find out, or try to find out. Also, anything known to anybody—the FBI might help there—about a vigilante group somewhere in the West, perhaps Missouri or Arkansas, which called itself "Patriots United." A Klan-like sort of thing, as nearly as

Heimrich could make out. Yes, Heimrich realized that all this would take time and might lead nowhere. Yes, he realized that there were papers which needed his signature. He would try to get in later in the afternoon. Lieutenant Rayburn had his doubts about a suicide in Harrison? Lieutenant Rayburn should continue his efforts to confirm or dispel them. Heimrich put the telephone in its cradle.

Lieutenant Forniss had checked in, Arthur told him. Forniss would meet the inspector at the Maples Inn. He had sent Crowley to the Powers house to find out what he could there.

"Pick up Mr. Olmstead's stallion?" Heimrich asked Arthur.

The pesky beast was still on the loose. He had last been sighted trotting south on Hayride Lane, dragging his tether.

Forniss was in the taproom of the Maples Inn. He was at a table which would, at a pinch, seat three. He was in a position from which he could see both the entrance to the taproom and into the corridor bar, where there were three tables along the wall. Forniss had a glass in front of him.

Heimrich sat at the table and gestured and in due course had a glass in front of him. He listened.

"Man named Samuel Bennington was her lawyer," Forniss said. "Forthcoming about her will, as lawyers go. Whatever she left . . ."

Whatever she left was to be divided, but not equally, among six nephews and nieces. Forniss had a list of their names. Only one lived in the vicinity—a man named Donald Powers, who lived in White Plains. And, for what it was worth, Donald Powers got half of the real and personal property of Faith Powers, deceased.

Bennington had no idea, he had told Forniss, what Mrs. Powers's estate might come to. Her broker would know that, or the banks would know.

"Banks aren't forthcoming," Forniss said. "Tried the First National. Talked to another Bennington. A V.P. Noises about a court order, like always. Seem to be a lot of Benningtons around here."

"Yes," Heimrich said. "One of them apparently collects garbage."

Mrs. Powers had owned her house and its ten or so acres free and clear. Samuel Bennington knew that because he had advised her as to where to file her mortgage discharge from a savings and loan association. At a guess, the asking price on the house would be in the neighborhood of fifty thousand dollars. Whether it would bring that was, in Bennington's opinion, a considerable question.

"Thing is," Bennington told Lieutenant Forniss, "this damn club is going to bring property values down. If it goes through."

"Say anything about Thomas Peters? Who's active in organizing this club?"

"That Peters is a notably able lawyer. That he can't really understand why a man of Mr. Peters's calibre would want to live in a remote rural area such as North Wellwood."

Forniss had gone from Samuel Bennington's office, on the second floor of a building on Main Street, to the offices of the North Wellwood Savings Bank, where Bennington told him he might find Lawrence Finch, who was not only Mrs. Powers's broker but the executor of her will.

"Probably be there today," Bennington said. "Since it's Tuesday. It's Monday and Wednesday Larry goes to New York. Has a brokerage office there."

Forniss found Lawrence Finch at the savings bank, behind a desk plate lettered LAWRENCE FINCH, VICE-PRESIDENT.

Lawrence Finch was a big man. Standing behind his desk and reaching a hand across it to Forniss, he was a portly one. He had a ruddy face and now it drooped. He shook his head sadly and said it was terrible, terrible about dear Faith. He said it was, frankly, hard to believe. That anyone would want to harm so charming a woman . . .

He said, in short, most of the things Charles Forniss had heard from other lips on similar occasions. Finch said that anything he could do to help. Anything . . .

"We're trying to find out where Mrs. Powers was going when she was shot," Forniss told him. "That among other things."

"She drove around a good deal," Finch told him. "Just to drive around. She loved that car of hers. It was—it was a toy as much as it was transportation, I thought sometimes. She drove it too fast. When I first heard I assumed she had driven off the road. It's a little tricky just there. I've been trying for years to get the town to put a decent guard rail. Perhaps now it will."

"It wouldn't," Forniss said, "have made any difference in this case. Mrs. Powers was dead, or as near as made no difference, when the car went into your gravel pit, Mr. Finch. I understand it is yours?"

"Yes," Finch said. "There's a good vein of gravel through there. There's a good demand for gravel, now the community is growing. Although whether with this club they're talking about ——" He shrugged his heavy shoulders.

"Apparently," Forniss told him, "Mrs. Powers made a telephone call from the inn. She was there with Professor Brinkley, we understand. He was the last person to see her alive, far as we've been able to find out. Says, the professor does, that she got into her car at some time after nine and then got out of it and said she had to make a telephone call. Like to know who she called, of course."

Finch could see that that might be important. He wished he could help about that. About anything.

"She wasn't, then, on her way to see you? When she was killed?"

"No. At any rate, I didn't expect her. Chances are she'd merely been driving around and was on her way home. Our road—Long Hill Road—leads into South Lane, you know. And then intersects Hayride Lane. As I said, she drove around a lot. Just to drive around."

"Way it looks to us," Forniss said, "somebody knew about where she'd be and about what time. And waited for her with a rifle."

"It couldn't have been an accident? Somebody trying out a new rifle?"

"Yep," Forniss said. "Could have been. Hell of a place to try out a new rifle. Any rifle, come to that. On a public road in pretty much the middle of the night. Still have to look into it, the police do. Start, like always, by trying to find out who profits. Reason I'm bothering you, Mr. Finch. Taking up your time."

Finch waved that off.

"I suppose you mean who inherits," Finch said. "Man to see about that is Sam Bennington. He was her lawyer. Drew up her will."

"We know who inherits," Forniss told him. "Bunch of nieces and nephews, Mr. Bennington says. And that you're the executor of her will. And have been her broker. Matter of fact, it was Mr. Bennington suggested I bother you. Thought you might be able to give us at least a rough idea as to the size of her estate."

"She wasn't a rich woman," Finch said. "General idea around is that she was, I suppose. Driving a Mercedes. Taking long trips to Europe, as she did last year. A good deal of the time, come right down to it, she acted—spent—as if *she* thought she was a rich woman."

"A rough idea," Forniss said. "One of the things we like to know, Mr. Finch."

"Most of what she had left was in bonds," Finch said. "I've always kept them for her. In my office safe in town at the moment. Haven't got a list of them here. Get it for you tomorrow, if you like."

Forniss told him that that would be fine. Meanwhile, a rough idea?

"Probably around thirty thousand in securities," Finch said. "Maybe a little more. She'd sold a good many. Or I did for her. Had to to keep to our agreement."

Forniss said, "Agreement?" and waited.

Her husband, Arthur Powers, had left Faith somewhere around two hundred thousand in securities, most of them bonds. Finch would have to look up the exact amount, but it was somewhere around that figure. Say they paid 4 per cent, which most of them didn't. But say they did. Bring her in around eight thousand a year. She had felt she needed more—a good deal more.

"So," Finch said, "we arranged that I'd pay her twelve thousand a year, quarterly, and sell bonds to make up what the interest didn't cover. So that she'd live partly on interest and partly on capital. She said, 'I'm getting to be an old woman, Larry. We'll sort of space it out.'"

Finch hadn't liked it, he told Forniss. Nobody knows how many years are left, for one thing. He had tried to get her to at least buy an annuity so that she could be sure of something. She had decided against that.

"It might have worked out," Finch said. "I'm no actuary, but it might have. Only, the twelve thousand a year wasn't enough. She kept selling more securities—living off capital."

Finch sighed at that. He shook his head sadly at that. Living off capital was, Forniss decided, a heinous thing to do. It violated commandments.

"Cars," Finch said. "New one every year, damn near. Trips to Europe. And she just gave a lot of it away, Lieutenant. Contributed to the new library wing, for one thing. And to the rehabilitation of the civic center—the old Bennington mansion, that was. Gave it to the Civic League, Sam and R. A. did. When they couldn't sell it, I guess. Needed a lot done and Faith contributed a lot. Had to sell bonds to do it."

He paused to shake his head again.

"Come down to it," he said, "Faith was a dear person. Everybody thought that, Lieutenant. Loved her for being the way she was. But she had no head for business. That she didn't have. Used to argue with her. Talked myself blue in the face. Nothing came of it. She'd say, 'After all, it's my money, Larry. Arthur left it to me.' Wasn't anything to say to that, of course."

"Nope," Forniss said. "Wouldn't be, would there? We heard somewhere she was planning to invest in this club they're organizing. The one a lot of people seem to be against."

If she had planned to do that, Finch said, she hadn't told him. On the other hand, it would have been like her. If she had come to him about an investment in the club he would have tried to talk her out of it—tried like hell to talk her out of it.

"That," Finch said, "would have been about the last straw. Throwing her money away on a thing like that. Also, it wouldn't have made her popular."

Forniss said they'd gathered there was opposition to the club. Not that it was any business of the police, but how did Mr. Finch himself feel about the club?

"I'm not enthusiastic," Finch said. "Not for around here. Maybe it's an affirmation of brotherhood, the way Clay Foster puts it in that paper of his. I'd just as soon brotherhood got affirmed some-

[107]

where else. Way most of us feel. Those of us who've got a stake in the place, anyway."

"Mr. Bennington," Forniss said, "seems to feel it will affect property values. Said something like that in connection with the value of Mrs. Powers's house."

He stood up as he said that, and Lawrence Finch also stood up and again reached his hand across the desk. Forniss took it. It was a little pudgy, but the grip was resolute.

"You're damned right it will," Finch said. "Change the rural character of the whole town."

"More than a gravel pit on a pretty slope down to a brook?" Heimrich said, when Forniss had finished his account.

"Yep," Forniss said. "That's the general idea, anyway. I didn't bring it up, M.L."

"He was forthcoming, wasn't he?" Heimrich said. "Anxious to help."

"Seemed to be," Forniss said.

The taproom had filled gradually. Most of those who came into it were men and, Heimrich thought, local men—Main Street merchants in business suits; countrymen in jackets and slacks. (Most of the jackets were of tweed; countrymen have a well-grounded suspicion of May weather. Summer jackets wait until mid-June.)

Women came into the inn's small lobby and came in groups. But, for the most part, they went into the main dining room. Two waiters began, briskly, to carry trays of drinks from the bar, through the taproom, across the lobby. A good many of the drinks were pink.

Of the men who came into the taproom and found tables or stood talking at the bar, none resembled the thin dark man Brinkley had described. One of them was a tall, heavy man. "Mr. Finch," Forniss told Heimrich. Mr. Pederson, who might possibly be named Nagle, was running late for lunch, or eating it elsewhere.

Ann Martin came into the taproom and stood just inside it looking around. Behind her was a tall and noticeably bony man. He was bareheaded and his brush-cut hair was blond. He was deeply tanned. Eric Martin, back so early from his work in New Canaan?

Ann Martin saw Heimrich and smiled at him. She and the bony man walked into the taproom in the direction of a table at the end of it. But by the table Heimrich and Forniss sat at, Ann Martin stopped. Heimrich and Forniss stood up.

"This is Roy Strothers, Inspector," Ann said and "Inspector Heimrich of the state police, Roy. And ——" She looked at Forniss and Forniss said, "Ser—Lieutenant Forniss, ma'am."

"Mr. Strothers," Ann said, "is connected with the network, Inspector. An associate producer."

"I take it," Heimrich said, "that you changed your mind, Mrs. Martin? About taking the summer off?"

"I thought it over," she said. "Thought there might be a story here. Called the office and Stu Leffing thought maybe there might be. Not the murder, of course. No pictures in that. But—oh, how the town reacts to the prospect of an interracial country club. So . . ."

"So me," Roy Strothers said. "To have a look around and see how much of a fuss there is. We won't get underfoot, Inspector. Try not to, anyway."

Heimrich said he was sure they'd try. He did not add that he was equally sure they would not succeed, if they did decide to do a documentary about North Wellwood—about a quiet village shaken out of serenity and forced to a choosing up of sides. With, he was coming to suspect, neighbor set against neighbor. UBN would, if it moved in, give the town the jitters.

"Also," Ann Martin said, "Roy knows this man Nagle you were talking about. Interviewed him—when was it, Roy?"

It had been several years ago, when Roy Strothers had been working for a newspaper, not for a network; it had been on the West Coast and Strothers's newspaper had been trying to find out what, in fact, Patriots United was all about. Nagle had been elusive; others had spoken more freely about the intentions of Patriots United, and said that the organization's only purpose was to arouse Americans to the danger of communism and denied as malicious propaganda all rumors that the Patriots were stacking arms. Aaron Nagle had stayed in the background.

"I had a feeling he worked from there," Strothers said. "Probably manipulated from there. I was sure somebody was doing that. There was a feeling of that. I did run him down. He said he was only rank and file. That now and then he helped out the cause by writing in its behalf."

"You'd know him if you saw him again?" Heimrich asked the bony man.

Strothers thought he would. Thin-faced, dark-haired and wiry; dark eyes set rather close together in his narrow face.

"The man Mrs. Powers wondered about was like that," Ann said. "I thought—Roy and I thought—he might be having lunch here. But I don't see anybody who looks like him."

"Neither have we," Heimrich said, and Ann Martin and the bony man went to the table at the end of the taproom.

And Detective Ray Crowley came from the lobby into the doorway and looked around the taproom and then came to the table and pulled a chair out.

Crowley, who looked like and was dressed like one of the locals at the bar, shrugged the wide shoulders under the subdued tweed jacket, and said he was afraid he didn't have much.

He hadn't needed the key they had found, undamaged, in Faith Powers's charred handbag, which was under her charred body in the broken Mercedes. The front door of her house had been unlocked. Which didn't, of course, need to mean anything. A good many country people trustingly leave their doors unlocked. There were no lights on in the house, which might mean that Mrs. Powers had expected to be back in it before it was really dark. Country people do leave lights on in their houses when they go out at night.

In Faith Powers's desk he had found her current checkbook. It showed a balance of $5,414.79. It showed a deposit, on April third, of $3,000, source not identified. He had found her previous checkbook and, entered in it, a deposit of the same amount, on January fourth.

"Quarterly payments from Finch," Forniss said. "As per this agreement of theirs."

There was a passbook of the North Wellwood Savings Bank. It

showed a balance of $8,375.16. There were no recent deposits. There was, on March 16, a withdrawal of around six thousand dollars.

The checkbooks were of pocket size and Crowley had them in his pocket and took them out. He also had the passbook. The withdrawal had been for $6,396 and no cents. "Looks like she had a payment to make and knew the exact amount she wanted," Crowley said. "Didn't transfer it to her checking account, far as the checkbook shows. Probably bought something that cost $6,396. The new car, maybe? But a Mercedes would run to more than that, new."

"We'll dig around," Heimrich said. "Any list of securities?"

There had not been, in the desk where Crowley had found checkbooks and passbooks, and bank statements, which he had left in Heimrich's car. Nor in bureau drawers and a few other places which seemed likely. "It's a big house inside," Crowley said. "Bigger than it looks outside. Take time for a real search. Gin and tonic."

The last was to the waiter, who looked at two almost empty glasses and got a shake of the head from Heimrich and a hand cupped over his glass from Lieutenant Charles Forniss.

"Any sign anybody had been there before you?" Heimrich asked Crowley.

There had not been. Which did not, of course, mean that nobody had been—which meant only that nobody had taken the place apart looking for anything.

They ordered lunch and ate it, and other lunchers thinned out of the taproom and drinkers from the bar. And no thin, dark, narrow-faced man came into the taproom. Ann Martin and Roy Strothers pushed back their table and walked toward the lobby. As they passed the table where the policemen loitered, Ann smiled and Strothers flipped a saluting hand.

"Check out on this nephew in White Plains?" Forniss said.

"To keep things tidy, naturally," Heimrich said. "Job for Ray here. Also, don't you think, he might drop around and see the estate tax people? Have them dig out the appraisal for tax purposes of the estate of Arthur Powers, deceased—when was it about, Charlie?"

"About five years, according to Finch. The nephew's Donald

Powers, Ray. Lives on North Main Street." He gave the address on North Main Street in White Plains.

They watched Ray Crowley, detective, New York State Police, walk out into the lobby.

"Doesn't look much like a cop, does he, M.L.?" Forniss said.

"No," Heimrich said. "Good kid, all the same."

They waited on over coffee and cigarettes.

"Could be," Forniss said, "that our friend has skipped lunch. Could be he's on a diet."

"Or," Heimrich said, "gone across the street for a sandwich in the drugstore."

He poured more coffee into his cup and the waiter looked at him with resignation.

"Maybe Missouri," Heimrich said. "Maybe Arkansas. Happen to know anybody out that way, Charlie? Southern Missouri, at a guess."

It is always worth while asking Charles Forniss if he happens to know somebody almost anywhere because it so often happens that he does. This time, however, he merely looked thoughtful.

"Can't say I—" he began and stopped. "Happens maybe I do," he said. "Unless he's gone somewhere else. Used to be a man on one of the St. Louis papers. Correspondent in Korea when I was over there. Only St. Louis isn't really Southern Missouri, M.L. Eastern edge, more or less in the middle."

"Now, Charlie," Heimrich said. "Settle for what we have. You might see if you can get this man on the telephone. See if he knows whether our Mr. Nagle has come out of the background since Mrs. Martin's friend found him there. And whether, of course, he has some special reason for wanting to stay there. For not wanting to be recognized and identified somewhere else."

"Yep," Forniss said. "Here. By Mrs. Powers. Worth trying, could be."

"Yes," Heimrich said. "There's a booth in the lobby, Charlie."

IX

THE PLANT OF the North Wellwood *Sentinel* was a low brick building at the end of one of North Wellwood's few side streets. The
street was Clinton Street and the houses on it were smaller and closer
together than on the other streets Roy Strothers drove the UBN
car through in search of the *Sentinel*. On Clinton Street the houses
were not so freshly painted as on Main Street. There were small children chasing each other along narrow sidewalks on either side of
the narrow street, and into the street. The children were, for the
most part, Negro. Strothers crept the car along the street. The
car had UNITED BROADCASTING NETWORK lettered large on either
side.

THE NORTH WELLWOOD SENTINEL, *Clayton Foster, Publisher* was
lettered on the door of the low brick building. So were the words,
JOB PRINTING. A pleasant-faced youngish woman behind a counter
wanted to know what she could do for Ann Martin and Roy
Strothers. Told, she said that Clay was up to his ears. But . . .

Clayton Foster's office was small. He and a desk and a typewriter
were alone in it, and the typewriter—on which he used two fingers
of each hand—was making a clatter. "With you in a minute," Foster
said, and kept on clattering. There were two wooden chairs, their
backs to a wall, and they sat on the chairs and looked at the editor
and publisher of the North Wellwood *Sentinel* who looked intently
at the keyboard of his typewriter.

He was a very thin man, in a white shirt, collar unbuttoned and
sleeves rolled up. He had a long face and no hair to speak of, and
it seemed to Ann that he and the typewriter vibrated together.

He reached the bottom of a page and yanked paper out of the
typewriter and whirled to his desk and began to read copy on what
he had written. He drew a heavy line through part of a sentence.
He wrote a word above one line and gave it a caret below. He got

up and said, "With you in a minute," and went out of the office. He was back in less than a minute. He said, "Now," and waited.

"UBN," Strothers said. "My name's Strothers. This is Ann Martin —Mrs. Eric Martin."

"Item about Mrs. Martin," Foster said. "And her husband. Taken the Barnes place. Oh. You're Ann Langley." He looked intently at both of them.

"All right," he said. "What's up your sleeves?"

Strothers told him what was up their sleeves, or might be.

"The town won't like it," Foster said. "Wants to be left alone, particularly right now. I suppose it's about this club?"

"The feel of the town," Strothers said. "About the club, of course. The opposition to it."

"And poor Faith Powers?"

"If that comes into it, Mr. Foster. Do you think it does?"

"There's an Inspector Heimrich working on it," Foster said. "And a Lieutenant something or other. Seem to be interested in her financial setup. At least this lieutenant is." He snapped his fingers.

"Forniss," Ann said.

"Seen her lawyer about her will," Foster said. "Talked to Larry Finch, who was her broker. Hasn't anything to say to the press. Which is me until the boys get up from town. Which ——" He broke off to look at the watch on his wrist. "Which ought to be any time now. Afternoons seem to be relying on AP. Which, at the moment, is me. *Times* has a couple of men on the way and I'm standing by for them. I'm a stringman for the *Times*. Stringman for damn near everything, come to that. A stringman ——"

"Mr. Foster," Roy Strothers said, and his voice was low, with just a hint of impatience in it, "I'm forty-five years old. I've been a newspaperman for more than twenty of them. I know what a stringman is."

And then, suddenly, Clayton Foster laughed. His laughter was unexpectedly gay.

"I'm sorry," he said. "We go to press tomorrow night. Getting the run on the two last sections started this afternoon. It's a small-

[114]

town weekly, Mr. Strothers . . . Mrs. Martin. This time every week I get jumpy about it."

"I always get jumpy," Strothers said. "It's a jumpy occupation. The feel of the town? You'll know, if anybody."

"Jumpy too," Foster said. "And don't I know. Last issue, we ran a story about the club on the front page. And about the opposition to it. About this open letter from the Preservation Association. See that, either of you?"

"Both of us," Ann said. "There was one of them in my mailbox yesterday. I've shown it to Roy."

"Impartial, our story was," Clayton Foster said. "Only impartiality isn't prized very much most of the time. Every group wants a newspaper to be impartial on its side. Also, I wrote an editorial, same edition. Favored the club. As—what did I say?—as an experiment in brotherhood. Walt Brinkley jumped me about that. Said that 'brotherhood' had got to be a mushy word. Said it was a pity, but there it was. Very interested in words, the professor is."

"Others jumped you for other reasons?" Roy Strothers asked the thin, vibrating man.

"You're damned right. Cancellations of subscriptions. Letters from the ones who always write letters, but more of them. Telephone calls. Some of them from people who've known all along I'm a Communist. That I've tried to cover it up by taking a stand against this black power thing, but that now I've shown my true colors."

"None for you? In favor of this club?"

"Some. Quite a few, actually. One thing I tell myself. People who are civilized—tolerant—they're not the ones who write letters. Make telephone calls. Which, before you say it, is being impartial on my side. The way ——" He broke off and looked rather sharply at Strothers and Ann Martin.

"You too," he said. "This documentary which stirred up the dear old Southland. Not much of which got to see it, of course. You both worked on that?"

"Yes," Strothers said. "Very impartial, we thought it was."

Foster laughed again.

"You take the point," he said. "It's sharper for the editor of a small-town weekly. On the other hand, our readers forget. Something else comes up. Traffic light at Main and Clinton? Waste of the town's money? Or vital to our growing community? Extension of Interstate Seventy-six through the west part of the township? Is the *Sentinel* to stand idly by?" He paused again. "A lot of clichés in our trade, Mr. Strothers," he said. "Coming in and, I'm afraid, going out."

But just now it was the interracial club?

Just now it certainly was. There had been an open hearing the week before, held by the Zoning Board of Appeals. Clayton Foster had covered it; it had been, he told them, a doozy. Most of those who spoke, and in a good many cases yelled, had been against the club. "Talked like this open letter from the Preservation Association, only a lot more so, some of them. Talked about black power. Talked, one or two of them, about 'niggers.' Not a word one often hears around here. But, again, it's the violent ones who go to town meetings, usually. The moderates stay at home and look at TV."

"Nobody for it?"

"A few. A chance for the Town of Wellwood to take a stand for decency and tolerance. Faith Powers, the poor dear, said something like that."

"The board itself?"

"Took it under advisement, of course. Thanked everybody for their interest, Sam Bennington did. He's the board's chairman. Said that he knew that if a few rather extreme statements had been made, they were made in the heat of controversy and represented only the deep concern of the speakers for the town's welfare. Very soothing man, Sam can be when he wants to."

"Will the club get its permit, do you think?"

Clayton Foster shrugged his thin shoulders, a little elaborately. He said he didn't know, couldn't make any informed guess.

"Five men on the board," he said. "All Republicans, of course, or they wouldn't be there. All conservative in outlook. Probably all five of them voted for Goldwater. Would again if they had a chance. This Election District went for him, incidentally. A bit lonely, even in Westchester."

[116]

"That will determine the board's attitude? This conservatism. Desire to keep things the way they've always been?"

"That," Foster said, "is what I don't know. They're all, I think, damned honest men. Of course, it's true that none of them, as far as I know, owns property near the Craig estate, where the club will be. They're all interested in the town, or they wouldn't be on the board, which has these meetings at eight o'clock in the evening. Sam himself likes a late dinner."

"Somebody," Ann said, "dumped garbage on our driveway last night. And let the air out of our car's tires. Some people in North Wellwood play rough, don't they?"

"Some in every town," Foster said. "Our share of riffraff. See the *Sentinel*'s police log. You tell the police?"

"Inspector Heimrich," Ann said, and was told it was a job for the locals. Not that they could be expected to do much, except perhaps to talk to a few of the resident hoodlums. Foster asked Ann for details, and was given them, and made notes. She told him about the two telephone calls, apparently intended for different people.

"Don't get that," Foster said. He looked thoughtfully at the ceiling.

It fell on him.

The ceiling fell on Clayton Foster, sitting at his desk. It fell to its own crackle and brittle bang and to the crash of an explosion. The low brick building shook violently. Glass clattered to the floor from the two windows in the office. The floor itself swayed under them; Foster's typewriter stand shook itself violently and crashed over, the typewriter thudding heavily on the heaving floor. A second section of plaster fell from the ceiling, crumbling as it fell. A solid piece of it banged, for a moment numbingly, on Ann's right shoulder.

Foster slumped on his desk, and blood began to run from his bald head.

Strothers went toward him, but before he could take the two steps across the room, Foster sat up. He said, "All right." He didn't sound it.

The door to the office had sprung open with the blast. Beyond it there was the sound of feet pounding on floor boards, and a woman screamed, her scream high and shaking.

Foster started to pull himself up from the desk and a heavy-set man with blood on his hands ran into the office. He wore a square cap, folded from newspaper. He said, "Jesus Christ, Clay. Jesus Christ! I switched on Number Two and Jesus Christ!"

"The others in the pressroom?"

"O.K., I guess. Blast knocked Billy down, but he got up again. Got up and got an extinguisher because some paper caught. But he got it out. Only, Clay, the press is sure as hell a mess. You're bleeding, Clay."

Clayton Foster looked down at the top of his desk and blood was dripping on it—dripping on broken plaster, into plaster dust.

"Well damned if I'm not," Foster said, and got a handkerchief out of a pocket and began dabbing his head with it. Then he said, "You two?" to Ann and Strothers. Ann had her left hand clasped on her right shoulder.

"All right," she said, and Strothers said, "Not a scratch. Looks like being a booby trap, doesn't it?"

Foster began to spin the dial on his telephone. After a moment he said, "Teddy? Clay Foster. Somebody's just blown us up."

Forniss was in the booth for more than fifteen minutes, and Heimrich waited at the table and said, when asked, that yes, he could do with some hot coffee. The waiter looked gloomily surprised but said, "Right away, Inspector," and went to get hot coffee.

Forniss came out of the telephone booth and, when he was in Heimrich's line of vision, began to nod his head. He came to the table and sat at it. He picked up the coffeepot and shook it and put it down again.

"More's coming," Heimrich told him. "I take it your friend was still on the paper?"

"City editor, now," Forniss said. "And knows quite a bit about our client, if he is our client. Nagle. Seems . . ."

It seemed that Aaron Nagle was, along with two other men, under indictment for a murder—a fatal beating which the Missouri

State Police were calling murder—committed in a small town in extreme southern Missouri. The victim had been the minister of the Methodist Church. He had been active in the civil rights movement. He had preached about it. He had also joined a "freedom march" in the deeper South.

"Deeper?" Heimrich said. "Missouri's a border state, isn't it?"

"Asked about that," Forniss said. "Seems there's this panhandle. Stretches down the Mississippi for a hell of a long ways, Langdon tells me. Langdon's the guy I know. Runs farther south than Kentucky. Southern state line, he says, is about the latitude of Nashville, Tennessee. Langdon says they call the panhandle 'Little Dixie.' Missouri, he says, was one of the first former slave states to desegregate its schools. Proud of that, most of the state is. But this Little Dixie section is sore as hell. The man who was killed lived in a town about as far south as you can get and stay in the state."

The clergyman who had been killed had been a native of the panhandle, but had been educated outside it. He had asked for assignment to the church in his home town. He was married and the father of a small son. He had been killed in the parsonage, where he had been baby-sitting and working on his next Sunday's sermon. His wife had been at choir practice. He had been beaten to death, apparently at about nine o'clock of an early spring evening. His name had been Lester Brown. He ——

Forniss was interrupted by a harsh hooting which seemed to fill the room. It was a rasping, mechanical sound, blasting at fixed intervals.

"Local fire department summoning its volunteers," Heimrich said. "Go ahead, Charlie."

Brown had reported to the sheriff's office the receipt of several threatening letters, telling him to get out of town or else. They were anonymous. They contained, in addition to threats against Brown, threats against his wife. There had also been a number of telephone calls. Brown had not thought they came from local people; thought the accent different. "They talk Southern down there, Langdon says. Whoever called Brown didn't."

"Nagle? How did they tie him in?"

That was not very clear, according to Forniss's city editor. The state police had taken over; they were clamming up. They had, evidently, got enough for an indictment against Nagle and two other men. One of the men had been a local farm worker. The other had been from Arkansas and had been a house painter, not then working at it. Both were in jail. Where Nagle was nobody knew.

How they tied Nagle into it was, again, a little vague. Langdon had had two reporters working on it. As nearly as they could find out, three men had turned up in the town the day Brown was killed and put up at a motel. They were, or seemed to be, just driving through.

"Only, Langdon says, through to where? Because this town isn't on the way to anywhere much."

They had been driving a car with Illinois plates. They had stopped at the motel in early afternoon.

"Apparently," Forniss said, "somebody recognized Nagle. State police aren't saying who, maybe because it wouldn't be healthy for whoever it was to be named. Or the state boys think it wouldn't. Langdon thinks, from what his reporters found out, it was the man who runs the motel. It was he, all right, who had noted down the license number of the car. He told the reporters he always did."

The car had been picked up the next day. It was heading north, toward St. Louis. There were only two men in it. There were two shotguns in the car and a .22 repeating rifle. The men said they had been shooting ducks. There were no ducks in the car.

They did not deny they had been at the motel the night before. They had checked in early in the afternoon because they had been up before dawn waiting—unsuccessfully, it appeared—for a flight of ducks. Subsequently, it had been established that the unemployed house painter from Arkansas was a member of the Ku Klux Klan.

"They must," Heimrich said, "have had a good deal more than they're telling to get an indictment, wouldn't you think, Charlie?"

Charles Forniss said, "Yep." Then he said, "One thing Langdon's reporters found out, the letters the Reverend Brown got were typewritten. Could be the type matched up with something. And could be one of the men they caught did some talking. Anyway, they want Mr. Nagle."

"Now, Charlie," Heimrich said, "so do we, I think. Or Mr. Pederson. Who—it could be, couldn't it?—didn't want Mrs. Powers to put the finger on him. Ask him where he was last night at about eleven."

There was a small telephone switchboard in the lobby and Mrs. Sally Lambert was sitting at it. Certainly, there was a telephone in Mr. Pederson's room. There were telephones in all the rooms. But Mr. Pederson did not like to be disturbed when he was working.

"Afraid we'll have to bother him all the same," Heimrich said.

"He won't like it," Mrs. Lambert said. "Came here to get away from telephones."

But she put a plug into its hole in the switchboard and moved a lever and, faintly, they could hear a telephone bell ringing above. It rang twice. Mrs. Lambert said, "Looks as if he's gone out." She was asked to ring the room again and shrugged at the absurdity of the request and rang the room again. Again there was no answer.

"Happen to know whether he came down to lunch today?" Heimrich asked her.

"Come to think of it," Mrs. Lambert said, "I guess he didn't. Not when I was in the lobby, anyway. And, of course, I'm there mostly at this time of day."

"He lunches here most days? Has since he's been staying here?"

"Of course," Mrs. Lambert said. "Meals go with the room." She looked at Heimrich and intentness settled on her spare face. "I do hope he's all right," she said.

They might, Heimrich told her, go up to his room and see. She didn't know, really. It was probably just that he didn't want to be disturbed. "He came here to work. For privacy. He ——"

"Now, Mrs. Lambert," Heimrich said, "I think we'd better have a look. Another key to his room? Or your passkey?"

"Oh," Mrs. Lambert said, "I'll go with you if you really have to make an issue of it."

She went ahead of them up the staircase which led from the lobby. She knocked at a door on the second floor and, when there was no response to that, said, "Mr. Pederson?" in a raised voice. Then she opened the door to a low-ceilinged room.

There was nobody in the room. There was the odor of cigarette smoke in the room. There was nobody in the small, somewhat antique, bathroom which opened from the room. There was a typewriter table in the room and a chair at it, but there was no typewriter.

The closet was as empty as the room. Using a handkerchief to cover his hand—not that that really did much good—Heimrich opened the three drawers of a clothes chest. There was nothing in any of the drawers.

"I hope," Heimrich said, "that Mr. Pederson didn't owe you rent, Mrs. Lambert?"

She was standing in the middle of the room, looking around it as if she expected her missing guest to materialize. She shook her head in answer to Heimrich's question. She said that Mr. Pederson was paid to the end of the week.

"Is it usual for guests to pay in advance?" Heimrich asked her. "Guests with luggage? I assume he had luggage?"

"A suitcase. And a portable typewriter. He wanted to pay in advance. I don't ask it."

Heimrich went to one of the corner room's two windows and looked out of it. He looked across Main Street. He went to the other and looked down into the inn's parking lot.

The police cars he and Forniss had come in were in the lot. There were four other cars.

If Roy Strothers of the United Broadcasting Network had come in a company car, Heimrich thought, the car probably would have had the network's name on it. If Henry Pederson—or, naturally, Aaron Nagle—had happened to be looking out the window when Strothers and Ann Martin parked their car and got out of it . . .

"I take it," he said to Mrs. Lambert, "there are back stairs? A way out which wouldn't take him through the lobby?"

"I just don't understand it," Mrs. Lambert said, speaking to the empty room. "Oh—yes, there are back stairs. And a fire escape, of course. But why ever ——"

Footfalls were heavy on the wooden stairs up from the lobby. A large policeman in uniform appeared in the doorway. He was a young policeman. What seemed to Heimrich a somewhat outsize revolver slapped at his right leg.

"Inspector," he said, "I'm Patrolman Bennington. Local police. Somebody's blown up the *Sentinel*."

X

THE PLANT OF the North Wellwood *Sentinel* was, Heimrich thought, more shaken up than blown up. Its brick walls still stood. There was a fire truck in front of it and a car marked NORTH WELLWOOD POLICE. There was broken glass on the sidewalk in front of the building and glass dust. There was no glass in the front door and only shards in the two windows which faced the street.

Forniss pulled the state police car in behind the North Wellwood police car, which was behind the fire truck. As he and Heimrich walked to the door of the building, which was sprung open, glass grated under their shoes.

The outer office did not seem to be much damaged. The drawers of a filing cabinet gaped open. A door to an inner office was open and a policeman with sergeant's chevrons on his sleeve was on one side of a desk and a man in shirt sleeves with adhesive bandages crisscrossing a bald head was on the other. There was a good deal of broken plaster on the floor.

A woman who looked pale but undamaged was behind a counter in the outer office. She said, "Can I help you?" and her voice was as pale as her face. "There's been a little accident," she added.

"State police," Forniss said. "We heard there was a little accident. Inspector Heimrich. I'm Ser—Lieutenant Forniss, Miss?"

"Mrs. Foster," the pale-faced youngish woman said. "You want to see my husband? His forehead—his forehead is all cut. Sergeant Hunter is talking to him. Of our own police force. But if you want ——"

"Matter for the sergeant," Heimrich said. "At the moment, anyway. Mind if we look around a little? We happen to be here on another ——"

"Of course," Mrs. Foster said. "About poor dear Faith. Of course, Inspector. It happened in the pressroom."

She pointed to a door, which also was partly open.

They went into the pressroom. There were two rotary presses in it and, unexpectedly, one of them was running. The already shaken building shook further as the press pounded, spewed cut-and-folded newspaper sheets methodically onto a slowly moving belt.

There were four men who wore fireman's hats in the room. They had a hose with them, which they had evidently brought in from the rear of the building. They had, as evidently, used the hose, although now it was limp on the wet floor. They were looking at a second press, which wasn't running and did not, to Heimrich's eyes, look as if it soon would run again.

A man who wore a fireman's hat, although a civilian blue suit, turned to them. He had the word CHIEF prominently on his hat. He said, "Want something?"

"State police," Heimrich said. "Having a look around. The press took quite a beating, didn't it?"

"You people taking over?"

"Now, Chief," Heimrich said. "Not on this. Unless it ties in with murder. Mrs. Powers's murder."

"Hell of a thing, that," the fire chief said. "Nice woman. Hell of a nice woman. Nothing to do with this, I'd think. Thing is, Clay Foster made somebody mad. He made a good many people mad, come to that. Coming out for this damn club, for one thing. On the other hand, couple weeks ago he put a blast on this black power thing. Niggers who want to kill all the white people. Could be somebody decided to start with Clay."

"With his plant, apparently," Heimrich said. "Some sort of booby trap?"

"Way it looks. Wired into the switch that starts the press. Way it looks. To us and to Ted Hunter. Dynamite, way it looks. Still smell it when we got here. You people got something like a bomb squad?"

"Something very like it," Heimrich told the fire chief. "We'll bring it in if the local authorities ask us to, Chief."

He wasn't, he thought, going to like the chief of the North Wellwood Fire Department. Which wasn't going to matter.

[126]

"Anything to show how they got in?" Forniss asked the fire chief. "And when?"

"Jimmied the back door, looks like," the chief said. "Listen. Whyn't you go talk to Ted Hunter? He's in charge of that side of it, isn't he? What we do is put out fires."

"Was there one?" Forniss asked him, in a tone which indicated that he didn't like the fire chief particularly, either.

"Could have been," the fire chief said. "Meaning to say we don't know our business?"

We're outsiders, Heimrich thought. Therefore, we merit hostility.

"No," Forniss said. "Nothing like that, Chief."

The fire chief did not answer him. He turned away and said to the other firemen, "All right, boys. Let's get her rolling."

Two of the firemen began to lug the limp hose out through the back door of the pressroom. Mrs. Foster appeared at the other door. She said, "You're wanted on the telephone, Inspector. It's Bobby Arthur."

Trooper Arthur told the inspector, in official language, that Barracks was fit to be tied; that things were piling up that an inspector was needed to unpile; that the District Attorney of Westchester County was one of the things, by way of three telephone calls. (Susan was not the only one, Heimrich thought, who felt that an inspector's job was a desk job. In the end, Heimrich thought, I'll have to get used to it.) He told Arthur to call Barracks and promise them an inspector within an hour or a little more.

Forniss had come out of the pressroom and was talking to the policeman with chevrons on his sleeve. The man with the bandaged head was fingering jammed keys of a typewriter. Heimrich silently wished him luck with it and told Forniss that he was going along to the Barracks and would leave the car at the Maples Inn. "So," Heimrich said, "it's all yours for now, Charlie." He thought that over for a second. An inspector was supposed to delegate. "I mean it's all yours," Heimrich said, and went out to the car.

At the inn, Sally Lambert was no longer behind the switchboard. Nobody was. Beyond it there was a door marked OFFICE and Heimrich knocked on the door. Mrs. Lambert said, "What is it now?"

Heimrich said, through the door, that it was Inspector Heimrich and that there were a couple of points. There was the sound of movement in the office and the door opened, a little violently. Sally Lambert's face, which was austere by conformation, was now, Heimrich thought, austere also by intention. She said, "I've got things to *do*. When am I going to get to do them?" But then she said, "Oh, come in I suppose."

Heimrich went in to a small office. A few points ———

Harry—Harry, not Henry—Pederson had been at the inn since three weeks ago the previous Sunday. As she had kept telling Heimrich, Mr. Pederson said he was a writer and wanted a quiet place to work for a month or so. Perhaps for longer. He had a suitcase and a portable typewriter and he had come in a Chevrolet, which looked new and which, she guessed, was rented. The car had New York license plates. No, she had not taken down the number on the plates. Why should she? Pederson had registered as from New York City, given no street address. He had made, during the three weeks, perhaps half a dozen long-distance telephone calls. All but one of them had been to New York City numbers. One had been to St. Louis. She had not made any record of the numbers called. Why should she? Of course she had asked the operator for charges. Mr. Pederson had paid them. Mr. Pederson had not made any local calls through the switchboard. If he had made any he had made them from the booth in the lobby. Yes, she thought he had used the booth from time to time.

"Did you hear his typewriter clattering a good deal?" Heimrich asked her. "I remember we could hear the bell ringing from here when you tried to call him."

"Mornings a lot," Sally Lambert said. "Not so much in the afternoons."

"Go out much in his car?"

Did he think all she had to do was to watch whether guests used their cars?

"He ate most of his meals here?"

"All of them, pretty much. We sent his breakfast up, because the dining room doesn't open until noon. He had lunch and dinner in the taproom, at the same table when it was available."

"Get acquainted with other people who eat here regularly? Local people? Probably a good many of the same people come in for lunch pretty regularly. Did Mr. Pederson seem to know any of them, or get to know them?"

"Am I supposed to be the FBI? Why are you so interested in Mr. Pederson, anyway?"

"Now, Mrs. Lambert. Partly because he seems to have been interested in not talking to me."

"You don't know that was it," Mrs. Lambert said. "Writers act funny, from what I hear. Do things on impulse. How would he know you wanted to talk to him?"

There was hostility in her voice, Heimrich thought. Merely the exasperation of someone interrupted when she had things to do? There were probably a good many things to do when one ran an inn. But was the hostility of another kind—did it match, say, the evident hostility of the fire chief? A hostility against intruders?

"I don't know that he did," Heimrich told the long-faced woman. "He could have seen our cars from his room if he had happened to look out the window. They aren't marked as police cars. But they have whip radio antennas. A man who didn't want to talk to policemen might recognize them. So Mr. Pederson didn't make any—call them bar acquaintances? Among local people—local men?"

"I told you ——"

"Now, Mrs. Lambert," Heimrich said. "I remember what you told me."

"He came here to get away from people," Mrs. Lambert said. "So he could work. Maybe he made what they call nodding acquaintances. I wouldn't know. Except with those fishermen, of course. I suppose just because they weren't going to be here except over the weekend. He did have drinks with them. Just happened to meet them at the bar, probably. And he had lunch with the blond one."

"Fishermen?"

Three men had asked for and got rooms at the Maples Inn the previous Friday evening. They had come in two cars, but they had seemed to be together. They had fishing gear in their cars. There was nothing unusual about it. A good many men checked in over weekends, using the inn as a place to stay while they fished "up towards Brewster." The three who had arrived Friday evening had got up early Saturday, having arranged for early breakfasts, and gone in one car.

"Bring any fish back with them? To be cooked here? I suppose your chef could have arranged that?"

They had not brought fish back, either Saturday or Sunday or Monday. Monday, only two of them had gone fishing. The other —the blond one—had stayed in North Wellwood. Come to think of it, he had pre-lunch drinks at the bar and Mr. Pederson joined him there. Afterward they had lunch together.

"These three. They're still here?"

They had checked out the night before.

Heimrich would like to see their registration cards. And also Pederson's card.

Mrs. Lambert got up from her desk, moving with indignation. She yanked open a filing cabinet drawer, using more force than she needed to. She slapped four cards down in front of Heimrich.

The names were printed on all four cards. Pederson had registered as from "NYC." A man named Robert Wilson and another named John Brown had been equally indefinite. William Snyder had put down Newark, N. J. The three fishermen, Heimrich thought, had notably usual names. Of course, what makes a name usual is its frequent use by those to whom it belongs. The name "John Brown," for example, belonged authentically to thousands—for all Heimrich could guess, to millions.

"I'll take these along," Heimrich said.

"I'm not sure you've got the ——"

"I am," Heimrich said, and put the registration cards in his pocket, handling them by their edges. He stood up and said he was sorry to have taken up Mrs. Lambert's time.

To this Mrs. Lambert made a sound which was a good deal like "yah."

[130]

Police Sergeant Theodore Hunter was sure the chief would want all the co-operation he could get from the state police. Experts from the bomb squad would be able to help a lot. It looked like having been dynamite—maybe two sticks and maybe three—wired into the press switch. Clay Foster had not been able to tell more than that the place had been blown up and plaster had fallen on him and that his typewriter was done for. There had been two people with him in the office—people from a TV network. A Mrs. Eric Martin, who had taken a house in North Wellwood, with her husband, for the summer. A man named Roy Strothers, who had come up, at Mrs. Martin's suggestion, to look things over. Neither had been hurt; neither had awaited the arrival of the police.

There was nothing more he could do there, Lieutenant Forniss decided—at least nothing more which was germane to his purpose, which was the apprehension of a murderer.

The telephone call Faith Powers had made after she and Professor Brinkley had finished dinner—made on a sudden decision after she had got into her car to leave. That might well be the crux of things; was a point for concentration. Only it was almost certainly an entirely blunted point.

If her call was local, that would be that. She would have put a dime in a slot and spun a dial with a finger. Nor, Forniss thought but was not certain, would there be a record of a call made outside the area from a public telephone. It would be made through an operator. When the proper number of coins had been pushed into a slot, that, Forniss supposed, would end matters. If Mrs. Powers had gone home and made a toll call from her own telephone, the number called would have been recorded for billing purposes.

Had she called someone to make an appointment? That was the most likely thing. Not Lawrence Finch, her broker, according to what he said. Not Thomas Peters, on the same evidence. Her lawyer, Samuel Bennington? (The village was certainly full of Benningtons.) He lived on Long Hill Road, not too far from where she was killed. For legal advice in more or less the middle of the night? Advice about some action she contemplated?

If she had called Bennington, and he—for some reason impos-

[131]

sible to guess—had decided it would be more to his advantage to kill than to advise he would, of course, deny having received her call. He would be given the chance. If she had called and Bennington had taken the call in the presence of a visitor and made a late appointment in the visitor's hearing? Bennington could be asked about that, too. There were a lot of people to be asked about a lot of things. The telephone company would be among them, on an outside chance.

Sergeant Hunter drove Forniss back to the Maples Inn. Heimrich's car was no longer in the parking lot. Forniss went to the booth in the inn lobby and dialed the business office of the New York Telephone Company.

The office of Mr. Samuel Bennington, attorney and counselor at law and also chairman of the Zoning Board of Appeals of the Town of Wellwood, was above a drugstore in a somewhat Colonial building on Main Street. It was nevertheless sedate. The desk in the outer office was firmly occupied by a middle-aged woman with her graying hair drawn back into a knot.

If Mrs. Martin didn't have an appointment, the receptionist—who deserved, Ann thought, a designation more formidable—didn't know. She very much doubted it. If Mrs. Martin cared to make an appointment for—tomorrow, perhaps? She thought tomorrow might be possible.

"I wouldn't take much time," Ann said. "If there isn't somebody with Mr. Bennington, perhaps . . ."

The middle-aged woman shrugged her shoulders firmly. But then she got up from her desk and went to a door behind it and knocked. A man beyond it said, "Yes, Grace?" She opened the door and went in. In less than a minute she came out again and a tall, gray-haired man in a dark gray suit came out after her. He said, "You wanted to see me, Mrs. Martin? Or should I say Miss Langley?"

He had a soothing voice and there seemed to be amusement underlying it. Everybody in this place knows everything about everybody, Ann thought. Information travels by some kind of osmosis. She said, "Either one, Mr. Bennington. I'll try not to take up too much of your time."

He did not say anything to that, but turned to the door and opened it and held it open. Inside, Samuel Bennington went behind his desk and said, "Sit down, Miss Langley," and Ann sat in a deep, leather-covered chair which seemed to engulf her. She felt as if she were sinking into it and peering up at Bennington out of some sort of cave. He smiled down at her pleasantly; he had, on the whole, a pleasant face.

"I assume," he said, "it's about this club?"

She thought of asking whether he read minds on the side.

"Your friend's car is quite plainly marked," Bennington said. "Faith's death, shocking as it is, is hardly, I'd think, an event to be covered by the United Broadcasting Network. For which you, Mrs. Martin are—what? An investigator? What would you title it, Mrs. Martin? 'Interracial club prospect shakes rural community'?"

"Interviewer," Ann said. "A shorter title, I'd imagine. But, yes, something like that. If Mr. Strothers and others higher up, of course, decide it's worth that kind of treatment."

"I," Bennington said, "would think it entirely too trivial for a network. I suppose as—what would you say, Mrs. Martin? An aspect of a larger problem? A part of the Negro revolution reaching into an unexpected place?"

He was tolerant; pleasant but tolerant.

"Mr. Bennington," Ann said, and tried to lean forward in the deep chair and decided that she would have to squirm unbecomingly to do that. She went on, from the chair's depth. "A white and Negro country club is revolutionary," she said. "In Westchester County. Actually, anywhere. Perhaps it is unique. I understand there is a great deal of opposition to it."

"In small places," Bennington said, "there is always opposition to any change. Matters which would seem entirely trivial to city people are magnified out of proportion. People hold meetings. Write letters to Clay Foster's newspaper."

"Which," Ann said, "has just been blown up. Because he supported the club, Mr. Bennington?"

"Senseless vandalism, I imagine," Bennington said. "Destruction for destruction's sake. By outsiders, probably. Some young hoodlums somehow laid hands on dynamite. I understand it was dynamite. Drove around the countryside looking for some place to blow up. Perhaps from Harlem."

"Do you believe that?" Ann asked him. "Really believe that?"

"That it was outsiders, yes," Bennington said. "Most certainly I believe that. Why, I don't know. That's a matter for the police, isn't it? That it had anything to do with the *Sentinel*'s support of the proposed club I doubt very much. We're not violent people around here, Mrs. Martin. Quiet people who want to live quietly."

"Mr. Bennington," Ann said, "my husband and I moved in yesterday to spend the summer in a quiet place. I met a charming, gentle woman and she was shot to death. Somebody dumped garbage at the foot of our driveway. Somebody let the air out of the tires of my husband's car. Roy Strothers and I are talking to the publisher of the local newspaper and the newspaper blows up. Living quietly?"

"Matter for the local police," Bennington said, and again spoke soothingly. "Or for this Inspector Heimrich. I gather you've met him. Very competent man, from what I hear. Just why did you come to me, Mrs. Martin? I'm an elderly small-town lawyer."

"And," Ann said, "chairman of this zoning review board. Which will decide whether to give the club a permit."

"So?"

"Mr. Bennington, just how widespread is the opposition to the club? And just how violent is it? You've read this letter against it. Signed by something called the North Wellwood Preservation Association. Exclamatory, the letter is. And not really about what it pretends to be about."

Bennington made loose fists of long, strong hands, and put them under his chin.

"I've read the letter," he said, and spoke slowly. "The broadside. I can guess, in general, who circulated it. I won't give you any names. But, for the most part, people who have moved in around here in the last year or so. Very aggressive, new people tend to be. Want to change things. Shake things up."

"You've got letters about this club? From these new people? Had pressure put on you?"

"Letters," Bennington said. "Telephone calls. Oh, I said there was opposition to the club, Mrs. Martin. There was opposition to Jay Noble's starting a riding school for kids. Too near a main road. Horses might get loose and do damage."

"Black horses?" Ann said, a good deal to her own surprise. And, also to her surprise, Bennington laughed. His laughter was brief. He said, when he had finished with it, that he doubted whether the color of the horses had much to do with it.

"You equate this riding school and the interracial club, Mr. Bennington? Expect me to believe you do?"

He seemed to consider that. But finally he shook his head.

"Perhaps," he said, "this is rather more extreme."

"The letters you got. They were unpleasant?"

"Some of them. The ones not signed."

"Did other members of the board get similar letters?"

He considered again.

"Roy Strothers is going around and asking them," Ann said. "I'm going to one of the others myself."

"Residents," Bennington said, "are entitled to make their views known to their elected representatives. Yes, I think all five of us have got letters. And telephone calls."

"All against the club?"

"Not all. Most, yes."

"Mr. Bennington, will the club get its permit?"

Bennington shook his head but not as an answer; as a deprecation of so ill-advised a question.

"The matter is under consideration," he said. "We ——"

Then he interrupted himself and looked at Ann with sudden interest.

"If the application is denied," he said, "it will make a better story, won't it, Mrs. Martin? Backlash reaches into a Northern rural community. Impartial survey, of course. Like the one you worked on about conditions in the deep South. Impartial with a tut-tut?"

"Impartial. If it's done at all."

[135]

"Make us look like bigots," Bennington said. "Prejudiced small-towners. No better, really, than what in the South, I understand, they call red-necks. Not a pleasant prospect for those of us who live here. Who are fond of our little, quiet backwater. To be made, come down to it, objects of ridicule. Even of contempt."

"Not by intention," Ann said. "We don't sensationalize."

"At best," Bennington said, "it would be a disruptive thing. I hope it isn't done. I very much hope it isn't."

"At UBN," Ann said, "I'm low woman on the totem pole. A man named Leffing will make the final decision. After, I suppose, a good many conferences. It will cost the network money, if they decide to go ahead with it. It won't, at a guess, pick up a sponsor. But ——"

This time she did manage to lean a little forward in the engulfing chair.

"If they do decide to go ahead with it," she said, "will you be interviewed? In front of a camera? Saying whatever you want to say, of course. Not to me. To a correspondent. Saying, if that's the way you feel, that it's much ado about nothing?"

He did not immediately answer. He looked intently at her across the desk.

"You are a key figure," Ann said.

"There are more important figures," he said. "Men better able to speak for the community. Larry Finch, for one."

"There's only one chairman of the zoning board," Ann said. "Oh, we'll interview others, if we interview anyone. Mr. Finch among them, I should think. I met him for a moment yesterday with Mrs. Powers. She said ——"

She had hardly known Faith Powers. It's odd, she thought, that my voice should break when I speak of her.

"That he owned half the town," Ann said, her voice steady again. "He laughed. Said it was not more than three eighths."

"Larry's a very influential man," Bennington said. "As to whether I'd be interviewed if, unfortunately, it comes to that. Yes, I suppose so. And say, probably, that it is a trivial disagreement among neighbors."

[136]

"Whatever you want to say."

She pulled herself up out of the deep chair and it was a little like pulling herself out of quicksand. She stood in front of the desk and Samuel Bennington, very long and lean, stood up behind it. Ann said it was good of him to have given her so much of his time and he said the meaningless words, "Not at all, Mrs. Martin."

"Speaking of Mrs. Powers," Ann said. "This is not for the network. At least, I don't think it is. You were her lawyer?"

"Yes."

"Did she ever say anything to you about investing in the club?"

"No."

"Say anything about the club at all?"

"Oh, she was in favor of it. She said that at a hearing we had about it. It was. . . ." And he hesitated. "The sort of cause Faith believed in. She may, I suppose, have thought of investing in it. They'll need a lot of money to get started."

"She didn't, though, say anything to you about investing?"

"I told you that. No. But. . . ." Again he hesitated. "She did, a few weeks ago, ask me what I knew about Thomas Peters. He'll head up the club corporation, if the permit goes through. He's a Negro, as probably you know."

"You told her?"

"What everybody knows about him. That he is a very able lawyer, as well as being a celebrated one. That I believe—that everybody believes, I think—that he is a man of complete integrity."

XI

M. L. HEIMRICH had advanced in rank, but rank did not carry the privilege of a larger office. INSPECTOR HEIMRICH was on the same door which had been lettered CAPTAIN HEIMRICH. The door opened to the same small office, and on this latish afternoon in latish May it was a very hot office. "Unseasonably warm," the forecast had been. "Chance of late afternoon or evening thundershowers." It was almost always unseasonably warm in the office, whatever the season.

There were more papers in the IN basket on the desk of Inspector Heimrich than Captain Heimrich had had to cope with. Heimrich took off his suit jacket and rolled up his sleeves and began to cope. He also began to answer the telephone. The District Attorney of Westchester County had been trying to get him all day. There was not enough for a first degree indictment in the case of the State of New York *vs.* Alexander Broskin. Maybe not even second degree, unless Heimrich could come up with more. And as for the case of . . .

It took time. It all took time. He could well, Heimrich thought, have spent the day at his desk. Another time, he would delegate, as an inspector should. There was no lack of competent men to handle cases. Charlie Forniss, for example, was a highly competent detective. He also knew somebody almost everywhere. He had got rather more about a man named Aaron Nagle and the murder of a clergyman in a small Missouri town than had come through channels. The Missouri State Police were inclined to be cryptic.

A technician came into the office with four registration cards, from which prints had been lifted. There were far too many prints. "Pawed over," the technician said, with disapproval. Some, because they recurred on all the cards, probably were those of the inn's staff. "Some are yours, Inspector," the technician said. Prints which were clear enough to read had been coded through to Washington.

son and by the three fishermen with whom, and it seemed only with whom, Pederson had struck up an acquaintance. They had got prints in the expected places in all three rooms. They had, as always, got too many prints.

"Lady who runs the inn, this Mrs. Lambert," Forniss said. "She's annoyed as all hell, M.L. Antagonistic. Think we were getting ready to tear the place down."

"Any special reason?"

"Wants to rent the rooms. Says if she doesn't make money this time of year when is she going to make it? I told her when the boys had finished she could go ahead and clean the rooms up and rent them. O.K.?"

"Now, Charlie. Naturally."

Forniss had gone to three of the five members of the zoning appeals board. The other two were commuters, still in New York or on their way out of it toward Brewster, via the New York Central. He had asked the three, Samuel Bennington being one of them, whether they had got protests against the club, and whether any of them had been violent.

"Because," Forniss said, "this blowing up of Foster's newspaper makes it look like there might be a tie-in. Mrs. Powers did, they all say, make a pitch for the club at this open meeting the board held. Must have been quite a meeting, from what they say."

All three had received letters and telephone calls in opposition to the club. Some of the letters and calls were similar, in tone, to the call to arms issued by the North Wellwood Preservation Association. A few of the letters, those anonymous, and one or two postmarked from out of town, were more violent. One or two of the telephone calls, those apparently local—"only you can't tell any more"—were threatening. One of the board members, a man named Notson, had been told he'd better watch his step if he didn't want anything to happen to his wife and kids.

"Notson's in real estate. Thinks he knows who made that call. A caretaker he fired. Says the man's a crackpot, which is what he fired him for being. Doesn't think it really ties in with anything, and could be he's right."

[142]

Both Bennington and Notson had been asked the same questions about the pressure being put on them before Forniss got to them—Bennington by Mrs. Martin, Notson by "this side-kick of hers," Roy Strothers. And when Forniss had left the house of the last man he had found at home, a car marked UNITED BROADCASTING NETWORK had drawn up in front of it and Strothers had got out of the car. He had flipped the approximation of a salute toward Forniss.

"One thing," Forniss said. "More a feeling than anything else, M.L. If this network moves in on the town it's not going to be any too popular. And it's not going to make Mr. Peters any more popular than he already is, which isn't very much."

"Tell the substation troopers to keep an eye on Peters's house, you think, Charlie?"

"Have," Forniss said. "They would have anyway, probably. Arthur seems to know his job. And the area."

And Forniss knows his, Heimrich thought. It is hard to delegate.

Forniss had "poked around" the village of North Wellwood, feeling the village out. At the local drugstore, he had bought aspirin he didn't need, and had said to the clerk, who turned out to be the store's owner, that he'd heard somebody had tried to blow up the local newspaper. The man had said he'd been afraid something like that might happen. And that it was a hell of a thing.

Forniss had talked to the postmaster, who also thought the attempt to blow up the *Sentinel* was a hell of a thing. Forniss had had a drink at the only bar in the town, except for the inn's bar. The bartender, who was also the owner, had thought it was a hell of a thing about the *Sentinel* and also about Mrs. Powers. Although he hadn't held with things Mrs. Powers and that professor had tried to put through when they were on the school board. Newfangled stuff, and he didn't want his kids subjected to it.

Forniss had gone to see a local general contractor. There he had asked about the club, which was, he gathered, going to need a lot of work done on it. The contractor had doubted if the club project would go through; had said the town didn't want it and said other, rougher things. He had also said that if it did, they'd sure as hell get somebody from out of town to do the work. He had also said that it was a hell of a thing about Clay Foster's press but that maybe Foster had asked for it.

Forniss had identified himself to the contractor, but not to the others—and there were a good many others—he had talked to as he poked around, getting the feel of things. One of the feelings he had finished with was that he had not needed to say that he was a lieutenant of the state police because that would not have been news to anyone. "Strangers stick out in a place like this."

The three fishermen had not stuck out. At the local hardware store Forniss had looked at fishing tackle and talked about—guardedly, since he knew very little of fishing—what luck people had been having along the Croton and in nearby reservoirs. He said three friends of his had been trying their luck around there over the weekend.

"Thought I might get a nibble. Nope."

"This contractor," Heimrich said. "Asked him for a guess on what the club's going to cost?"

"A couple of hundred thousand would be his guess," Forniss said. "Fifty thousand, anyway, to turn the Craig house into a clubhouse. The rest for the golf course, and wells and driveways and the lot. Lot of clearing to be done. And a lot of grading, if they were going to make it anything like a decent course. Said the driveways alone—because the zoning board, if it approves the project, will hold out for decent access and exit drives—would cost one hell of a lot. Gravel alone, if they decided to use gravel, would set them back good and plenty."

"Why gr—— Oh, sure enough, Charlie. Not too much of it around there?"

"Not in easy trucking distance, M.L. Which has sent the price per yard up. Two or three times what it was a few years ago, the man says. A lot of demand, with a lot of new houses going up."

"Nice for Mr. Finch," Heimrich said. "But you were way ahead of me on that, naturally. Of course, if he already owns half the town. Or even three eighths."

"Happens I went around to the Wellwood town house," Forniss said. "That's what they call the town hall. Mrs. Powers's house is tax appraised at twenty-five thousand. Seems the town appraises for taxes at half what they estimate the property would bring on the market. They assess land around here at fifteen hundred an acre."

"The twenty-five thousand includes both house and land?"

It included five acres of the land. An additional five Arthur Powers had purchased after he bought the house was a separate plot, separately assessed. At seventy-five hundred.

"I told Crowley to go into Barracks," Forniss said. "Tells me you've got a job for him."

"Car rental agencies," Heimrich said. "Mrs. Lambert thinks Pederson, or Nagle if he is Nagle, was driving a rented car. Perhaps his three fishermen friends were. Maybe under other names, naturally, because rental places look at driver's licenses. Could be Nagle, if he is Nagle, rented under his own name."

"Yep," Forniss said. "Unless he got his license under the name he's been using around here. Tomorrow I'll need Ray to help go over Mrs. Powers's house. Not that I know what we'll be looking for. O.K., M.L.?"

"Yes. While you were at the town house did you . . . ?"

"Yep. Mr. Finch does own a lot of the town. More than five hundred acres of it, a good deal of it bought within the last year or two. Seems he's a developer, among other things and it's a good time for developers around here. Town clerk says the population of the area —that's the town, not the village—has more than doubled in the past four-five years. Says most places within commuting range have."

"Quite a lot of land," Heimrich said. "At three thousand an acre. Mortgaged? Mr. Finch's land?"

"Nope. Anyway, they send the tax bills to him. Usual setup is, mortgage companies pay the tax bills, just to be sure they're paid. Up the mortgagor's payments to cover, of course."

"Sounds like a very solvent man," Heimrich said.

"Yep. Does at that. Incidentally, seems he wants to get even more solvent. Got a permit a few months back for another gravel pit. Same strip of land along the brook. Looked it up on the land map. This one will be just about opposite Thomas Peters's house. That's all I've got, just now. Only I think I'll get a room at the inn. Make some bar acquaintances tonight, if they'll make acquaintance with an outside cop. Expense account, M.L.?"

There is an advantage to being an inspector. "Yes, Charlie," Heimrich said. "Put it in and I'll see it goes through. Good poking around."

"Ought to be," Forniss said. "Some sort of shindig at the inn this evening. Rotary, Lions, Kiwanis—one of those. Set up in the main dining room. Speakers' table and everything. Most of the leading citizens ought to show up. Way I figure it, a lot of them will visit the bar before and after. Be talkative, maybe."

"Sort of thing that happens," Heimrich said. "Good listening. Have you ——" He stopped himself. It was Charlie's. Learn to delegate.

"Arthur and his side-kicks are going to do a good deal of cruising around tonight," Forniss said. "Out on Hayride Lane, among other places. Where your friend Brinkley lives. And where the Martins had taken this house. With their flashers going, shouldn't wonder. Making rather a show of it. You were going to say something, M.L.?"

"No, Charlie," Heimrich said. "Not a thing."

It was growing dark in Heimrich's office as he put the telephone back in its cradle. Automatically, he switched on his desk lamp. He reached again toward the telephone to call Susan; to tell her what she would certainly already know, that he was going to be late. That he hadn't realized how late it had got ——

He looked at his watch and withdrew his hand from the telephone. It was still a little before six. There ought to be, still, several hours of daylight—of saved daylight in late May. He went to the small window of his small office and looked out of it toward the west.

The sky was black where the sun should have been. As he stood at the open window he heard, far off, the rumble of thunder. Under the black clouds there was a still distant flashing. Moments later the thunder sounded again. A good way off, still; a good many miles up the Hudson Valley. Perhaps Van Brunt was already getting it. It looked like being a big one.

Three miles up the Taconic, on his way to Van Brunt, Heimrich

[146]

had to switch on his headlights. The whole of the northwest sky was black. Lightning slashed through the black clouds. It still did not rain. The storm held its breath.

As a storm of another kind held its breath in North Wellwood? The analogy was fanciful. What was going on in North Wellwood was not, looked at logically, obscure; looked at with the logic imposed by the times. A community which had thought itself secure from change, from intrusion by the world, was threatened with both. Because there was a chance that Negroes and whites might have a place to play golf and tennis together, swim together, eat together in a club dining room.

A woman had been shot to death on a lonely road and her car had plunged into a gravel pit. The plant of a small-town weekly had been damaged by a dynamite blast. There was no certain, or even probable, connection between those things. A man who might, or might not, be a member—perhaps a leading member—of a group of right-wing fanatics had left a hotel room abruptly, but not without paying his bill. Three fishermen had had no luck fishing. A television network might, or might not, intrude on a village which did not like intruders.

Of course, in New York City, the police had rounded up twenty or so men whom they accused of planning to blow up Communists, when found, and who seemed to have been equipped to do it. But those called themselves "Minutemen," not "Patriots United." Of course, the right wing, like the left wing, probably had splinters in it. Of course . . .

Heimrich was in The Flats, a few miles below Van Brunt Center, some five miles from home, when the storm quit its ominous holding in of breath. Lightning tore holes in the sky and water poured out of the sky; thunder shook the small, close houses of The Flats. The road ahead almost vanished in the downpour.

Heimrich put his lights to full, and saw only a wall of water. He dipped them and could dimly see the road, and he crept the car along it. He crept to Van Brunt Center, leaning forward over the wheel. The car was sluggish; Heimrich felt as if it were swimming uphill.

There were no lights in the Center, as Heimrich sloshed the car along Van Brunt Avenue, which is also NY-11F. The buildings on either side of the street were dark—dark as this sudden night in late afternoon. Even the Old Stone Inn was dark. It, like the other buildings, momentarily flashed into view as the lightning flashed. The traffic light at the Corners was out. Normally, Heimrich would have turned there, into Elm Street, then on to Van Brunt Pass. It was the short-cut home. But this was no night for the Pass.

He went on to High Road. Water rushed down as he turned into it, began to climb it. It was like trying to drive up a waterfall. The car's motor faltered for an instant and Heimrich moved his gear lever to L. He had never needed to use low gear before; the Buick's automatic transmission had always taken care of such matters. He almost missed his own driveway, but his lights dimly picked up the two boulders which flanked it and he crept between them and up the steep drive.

Power was off here, too. Electricity tamed to wires is no match for electricity leaping unfettered in the sky. The house was dark. Now, as he drove in front of it and into the garage, there were candles burning behind windows. There was flickering light in the house —light flickering red.

A breezeway connected garage and house. It was a galeway as Heimrich ran through it—was hurtled through it with a cold wind at his back. Down twenty degrees within the hour; more than twenty degrees from the feel of it.

The house door opened as he reached it and the wind blew him home. Inside, he leaned hard against the door but was not quick enough. Several of the candles flickered out. He stood for a moment with his back bracing the door and looked down at Susan, who wore slacks and a sweater; she looked up at him and said, "Not for man or beast, is it? I was worried, Merton. I—I hoped you'd stop some place until it was over. I . . ."

She was shaking when Merton Heimrich put his arms around her. She quieted in his arms.

"It's just a thunderstorm," he told her.

"It's fine now," she said. "Look."

[148]

She nodded toward the fireplace.

Colonel was lying, facing the fire, his forepaws stretched enormously toward it. And between the dog's great paws there was a small black curl. A head came out of it and rested on one of the paws and the curl became a small black cat.

"Colonel brought the mite in when he heard the thunder," Susan said. "You know how storms frighten him. Our cat didn't much want to come, but Colonel picked him up. Got him very wet all over again, of course. So I lighted the fire. I'll get us drinks."

But for a moment they stood side by side and looked at enormous dog and tiny cat.

"Colonel," Susan said, "thinks he's a papa."

XII

Summer storms grumble their way from west to east. The sun was still bright in North Wellwood at around six, when Ann Martin drove the little car—Eric's little car—up the drive toward the square white house. She drove up fast, with gravel spurting from under the wheels. Eric would be wondering what on earth . . .

Eric was not there to wonder. She was at once relieved and mildly concerned. The station wagon was never very resolute. It might have tired on its way from New Canaan. She left the sports car in front of the house and was on the porch when she heard the telephone begin to ring. It rang three times, but only three, before she reached it.

Eric was tied up at the plant; would be, at a guess, for another half an hour. So, in an hour or a little more. If the damned station wagon agreed to start. Eric Martin disliked the station wagon strongly; Ann sometimes thought that the wagon responded in kind.

"Roy Strothers is coming by for a drink," Ann said.

"Roy Str—— *Ann*. You haven't let them hook you? We agreed. I thought we'd damn well agreed."

"Things," Ann said. "All sorts of strange things, Eric. The nice Mrs. Powers I told you about. Somebody shot her. And somebody blew up the local newspaper and ——"

"And when I get there," Eric Martin said, "we'll load this damn wagon up again and get the hell out of there."

"Of course, darling," Ann Martin said. "Whatever you say, darling."

"And," Eric said, "none of that, my dear. You can skim the resigned acceptance off and throw it. At Mr. Strothers. No. Tell Mr. Strothers to go roll his hoop. And don't say, 'Yes, darling.'"

"No, darling."

He laughed then. He said, "Sometimes—" and did not go on with that. "I'll make it as soon as I can," he said. "Give Roy cooking sherry."

"I'll tell him what you said," Ann said. "And ——"

A car honked briefly.

"Somebody's here," she said. "Probably Roy. Come as soon as you can, Eric."

"Wait!" he said. "Be sure it is Roy. Not—not somebody delivering garbage."

She went to a window and looked out at a car marked UNITED BROADCASTING NETWORK and at Roy Strothers getting out of it. She went back to tell her husband that everything was all right.

"An hour," Eric said firmly. "Remember the cooking sherry."

"There isn't any," Ann told him, and hung up. She went to the door and let Roy Strothers in. Outside it was warm and hushed.

"There's a storm around somewhere," Strothers said. "Tried to pick up the six o'clock news on the car radio and didn't get anything but static. Does an enquiring reporter get a drink around here?"

She made them drinks, not from cooking sherry. They sat in chairs by an open window, through which no air came. Ann said, "Well, Roy?" and Roy Strothers sipped before he answered. Then he said, "I'd think so. But it's up to Stu. You?"

They had divided up interviews; they met now to compare notes before they called Stuart Leffing in New York. Ann told Strothers about her interview with Samuel Bennington and that Bennington, reluctantly, would consent to be interviewed if they went ahead with it. She had gone from his office to Lawrence Finch's house on Long Hill Road and found Finch relaxing on a deck chair in the shade and sipping a gin and tonic.

Finch said, sure, he knew there was opposition to the club. He wasn't for it himself. Not around there. Maybe it was all right in theory. Maybe a lot of theories were all right. The trouble was, come down to it, that a lot of people were trying to do things too fast. The people who were running things now in Washington were trying to cram things down people's throats. Had been for years. Inciting people, was what it came to.

"I'm a conservative," Finch told Ann Martin. "Most of us are

[152]

around here. Maybe we're a vanishing breed. Maybe this socialism they're pushing is what we're headed for, whether we like it or not."

"This club," Ann said. "You feel it's Socialistic? At—I heard the initiation fee was to be around a thousand dollars?"

She was sitting in a director's chair, in the shade of a big maple. She had been offered, and declined, a drink.

"It was peaceful," she told Strothers. "He didn't argue that the club itself was what he called socialism. Only that it was breaking down old traditions. But he wasn't violent about it. Resigned, on the whole. He talked a bit about property values going down. He said, 'All right, I own a good bit of land around here. So I'm not exactly impartial.' He thinks it's all not worth our making a fuss about. If Sam Bennington wanted to be interviewed in front of a TV camera that was up to Sam Bennington. He himself won't be, Roy. Says it's something he's not involved in."

"Would he show up all right on the screen?"

"Representing the better element, I suppose so. Big, impressive in a way. Banker type—what people think of as the banker type."

"Only banker I know to speak to is thin as a rail," Strothers said. "There comes our storm, honey."

There was the roll of distant thunder.

Ann had gone from Finch's big white house to the similarly big, and even whiter, house owned by Thomas Peters, attorney and counselor at law. And Negro.

"He's got a wife who's a knockout," Ann said. "Put a camera on her and it will open all its lenses wide. He's good-looking himself. Both very photogenic."

But—"We don't want that kind of publicity," Peters told her. "This isn't an issue. It's a club—a country club. We're not trying to prove anything. Not trying to stir things up."

"A woman's been shot and killed," Ann said. "A newspaper's been blown up, or part blown up."

There wasn't, Peters told Ann, any evidence—any real evidence —those things were connected in any way with the club. It was tragic about Faith Powers. She had been a fine woman. As for Clayton Foster, he got out a good newspaper. He was quite a guy. And

[153]

a good many people had grudges against him. The fact that the *Sentinel* editorially had supported the club might be completely irrelevant.

The thunder grew louder and closer and it began to grow dark in the living room. But still no air came in through the open window they sat by.

"If Stu does decide on this," Roy Strothers said, "will Peters play along? State his side of it?"

She didn't know. Peters would not commit himself.

"Can't very well play Hamlet without Hamlet," Roy said. "If it weren't for this booby trap at the paper I'd recommend to Stu that we skip it. And Peters is right, of course. We can't tie that in. Not hard enough, anyway. And Mrs. Powers we can't tie in at all."

"General unrest," Ann said. "Village in tension. Neighbor turned against neighbor."

"We'd have to pipe it," Strothers said. "Blow it up. And this I'll say for Stu. Simon Legree he may be, but he doesn't like things piped."

Strothers had talked to two of the five men on the zoning board —a man named Leonard Notson and a man named Ben Lacey. Both of them had received letters protesting the club; Notson had got a few telephone calls about it; Lacey said he had not.

"What you city people don't realize," Lacey told Strothers, "is we small-towners get easily steamed up about local matters. Because, I suppose, we feel we're a part of them in a way city people don't. Can't. So we blow off steam and things quiet down. If we're let alone."

"He wants us to leave it alone?"

"Both he and Notson. They ——"

Thunder, very close now, drowned out his voice. It rumbled itself away.

But then a sharp flash of lightning split the deepening darkness. Strothers waited it out.

Ann crossed the room to a light switch and flicked it up. A porch light went on. She tried another switch and three lamps went on in the living room. There was a roar of thunder and the lamps flickered, seeming to wince from the storm. But they came back steady.

[154]

"Going to be a big one," Strothers said. "Hope this husband of yours makes it home before it really breaks."

"So do I. How about you, Roy? Driving back to town?"

He was not. He had decided to stay over at the inn. Anyway . . .

Both the board members he had talked to hoped the network was not going to make a thing of it. If it did, they both supposed they'd have to be interviewed. Neither of them wanted to.

"One thing—" Roy said, and again was drowned by thunder. It was not a rumble this time. It was a crash. The lights flickered; then went out. It was abruptly very dark in the room. But then the lights came back on again.

"This Lieutenant Forniss," Roy said, in the momentary quiet, "seems to be making the same rounds we've been making. He'd talked to Notson before I got there. Notson wasn't explicit, but I suppose about the attitude of the town, as maybe demonstrated in the blast at the *Sentinel*. Whether it ties in with anything they're after."

"Inspector Heimrich," Ann said, "is after whoever killed Faith Powers. I suppose the lieutenant is too."

"Scope of the enquiry maybe's widened," Strothers said. "To use a tired phrase, as who doesn't? State police don't like people setting off dynamite charges. And Mrs. Powers seems to have come out in ——"

Lightning tore the premature dusk to tatters. Thunder was almost immediate and now it was sharp, shaking—seeming to shake the house. The lights did not flicker this time. They went out. Strothers said, "Damn!" and then, picking up a sentence, ". . . favor of the club. Made a speech about it at this open meeting, both Notson and Lacey say. And that it's ridiculous to suppose that her murder had anything to do with that. Notson said I had pretty crazy ideas about the town if I thought people shot each other because they didn't agree about something."

"Only, people do. I hope Eric's turned in somewhere. Or's stayed at the plant."

"Probably has. Yes, people do. But not, the idea is, in North Wellwood. Anyway, Lacey says, nobody's proved Mrs. Powers was murdered. Says too many people give kids guns before they're old enough to handle them. Not that he's against guns. He's a member of a local rifle club himself. Right to bear arms is guaranteed under ——"

Again the lightning ripped around them and thunder exploded.

"—the Constitution," Strothers said. "Noisy as hell, isn't it? Says the whole nation is getting soft, which is just what the Commies want. So, naturally, I asked him if he'd ever heard of a man named Nagle. Or of a gang—only I said 'organization'—which calls itself Patriots United. He said he never ——"

Again lightning leaped around the house and thunder cracked over it. Strothers waited it out.

Darkness was almost complete in the room. Their cigarettes were red spots, waxing and waning as they drew on them. Ann groped for an ash tray and found it and ground her cigarette out in it. There is not much point in smoking in the dark.

Still there was no wind.

"Tornado weather," Strothers said. "Out where I grew up this was tornado weather. We called it cyclone weather."

"Not here," Ann said. "Not this far ——"

Thunder drowned her voice. The house, which had weathered many storms, shook with the thunder.

"Wouldn't bet on it," Strothers said. "Over the state line, in Connecticut—not more than maybe ten-fifteen miles from here—the selectmen bet on it a few years back. Let the wind insurance on their new school lapse. Tornado came along . . ."

Again he had to wait for the crashing noise to cease.

"And," he said, "blew the roof off the new school. Very inconsiderate. And very untraditional. Tornadoes ought to stay in the Plains states where they belong. One thing about Notson. He got a phone call just as I was ready to leave. We were in what he calls his study and . . ."

The telephone on Notson's desk had rung and Notson had said, "Excuse me a minute, will you?" and picked it up. Strothers could hear the grating of a man's voice, but not the words. Notson said, "You mean tonight, Sam?"

The other voice grated again.

"Well," Notson said, "I guess so, if you put it that way. Although what the great rush is all of a sudden."

Again the other voice grated. Notson listened longer this time. Then he said, "How about the others?" and again listened.

"All right," Notson said. "If you say so. You're the boss. Nine o'clock it is."

Then he hung up.

" 'Sam'," Ann said. "And 'you're the boss.' "

"Seemed likely," Strothers said. "Summons from the chairman. Notson didn't expect ——"

Lightning flared in the room and the crash of thunder was instant. And then rain beat the house and the rush of wind was violent in it. Rain blew in sheets through the window they sat by.

"Windows!" Ann said, her voice raised above the tumult. "Help me get ——"

She started up from her chair. In the darkness, in a house strange to her, she stumbled over something. She caught herself as she was falling, putting both hands out against the wall. She heard Strothers say, "Damn!" and heard him move and bump into something. She reached toward the open window and something shot through it —an object like a ball, in shape and size. Something the wind had lifted from somewhere, hurled from somewhere? Something ——

It landed on the floor beyond her; clanged on the floor.

Then there was thunder again but the thunder was in the room. No, not thunder. Sharper. More ——

The room shook around her and was lighted by a violent flash. Not lightning. A flash of red and ——

Another object, like the first, came through the window.

Behind her, Roy Strothers cried out, his voice high—his voice a scream.

"God! I'm ——"

Then his voice stopped.

There was the red flash again. And then there was a blow on the back of her head—a violent, crushing blow. Then there was blackness.

[157]

Rain and wind shook the station wagon. Eric stopped its forward lumbering because the traffic light at the junction of South Lane and Main Street showed red. Then the light went out, but the green did not come on. He could look down Main Street and all the lights were out. He crept across Main Street, feeling his way toward Hayride Lane. Which ought to be . . . this was it . . . this was . . .

Cursing—cursing the weather and the clumsy station wagon—he backed out, through coursing water, from the driveway he had lumbered into, thinking it the beginning of Hayride Lane. He went forward again. Then he inched again to the right. If this wasn't . . .

It was a road, at any rate. Lightning leaped around the car. In the instant of its leaping a sign was visible through falling sheets of water: "Hayride Lane."

A couple of miles more, if the house hadn't blown away. If the road hadn't washed away. If he didn't get blown off the road; blunder off the narrow road. If he could find the driveway when he got to it.

There ought to be houses along here. There were no lights showing. Then lightning leaped again and on his right a house leaped out of darkness. The Powers house, if he was guessing right. Only not the Powers house any more. Ann had told him that. Life had gone out of the house.

Half a mile or so now, if he knew it when he got to it. A strange driveway on a strange and violent afternoon; an afternoon which flashed and leaped around him. It was raining so hard now, the rain beating so furiously on the wagon, that he could hardly hear the thunder. Yet the thunder shook the straining station wagon.

Here?

No, nothing here. Perhaps a momentary widening of the road. A stone fence beyond the widening. I don't remember a stone fence here, Eric Martin thought. I don't remember a damn thing about any of this. I'm lost. I'm sure as hell lost in ——

Again lightning served him. On his right a mailbox; beyond it the start of a driveway. His own—his own since yesterday? Or somebody's. It didn't matter. Somebody he could ask where the hell he was.

He turned up the driveway. In a lightning flash another house leaped into view. A big house with evergreens in a row in front of it. By God, Eric thought. By God, I've made it. I'm ——

There was, dimly in the dim lights of the wagon, movement in front of the house. The movement became a car. A car with no lights, yet one in sudden movement. It was moving down the drive; picking up speed on the drive.

Eric Martin leaned on the horn rim of the wagon. The wagon blared at the lightless car. The car kept on coming. Ann? *Ann going somewhere in this? With no lights?* But she could see his lights. Whoever was driving could see his lights. He leaned hard on the horn rim.

The approaching car began to pull toward its right, and Eric yanked the wagon toward the right. He felt its wheels go up on grass, begin to churn in grass.

The drive's too narrow, Eric thought. There isn't going to be room. Some crazy, bloody fool ——

The wagon shrieked, metal against metal. Eric was hurled to the side. His seat belt caught him. The wagon's lights went out. The wagon leaned far toward the right, but held there.

He pulled himself up by the wheel and tried the door. It was jammed. Lightning flashed again. The other car was lying on its side by the drive. Not the MG. Then, please God, not Ann. Then— Roy Strothers? He'd been there. Was supposed to have been there. He ——

Eric tugged his seat belt free and slid down the canted seat. The door was partly embedded in wet turf. No chance of forcing it open. He wrenched at the window crank and it stuck. He yelled at it, swore at it. And wrenched at it. And slowly, jerkily, it slid down. Down to a point where he could climb headfirst through it, get hands on soaked turf.

He crawled out from beneath the tilted car. After a little way he could stand up, bracing himself against wind and rain.

From beyond the other car there was a sharp flash, and then an explosion. A bullet clanged against the hood of the tilted station wagon.

[159]

Eric Martin ducked back behind it. There was the sound of another shot, but this time there was no clang of a bullet against anything.

There was another flash. There was now almost no interval between flashes of lightning. Lightning flared through the world.

In its flare, Eric saw somebody running from behind the prostrate car. It was a man; a man in a flapping raincoat. A slight man, Eric thought. He seemed to be blown by the wind behind him. He carried a revolver in his hand when he first started to run, but then, Eric thought, he thrust it into a pocket of the raincoat. He was running toward the road. Lightning failed and he ran into darkness.

Eric ran toward the house. There was no use in shouting through the tumult of the night, through the beating of the rain and the crashing of thunder. But as he ran up onto the porch of the house Eric shouted his wife's name. He kept shouting it as he pushed the door open.

The door hit something and stuck. He pushed harder and forced the door open.

Wind was sweeping through the room, carrying rain with it. There were no lights in the room. Then lightning flared through the windows.

The room looked as if it had been torn apart. A glass-fronted bookcase lay face down in broken glass. A mangled chair had blocked the front door.

The lightning failed again, but now it did not seem to be dark in the room. It was dim there, still, but the dimness was, suddenly, not much more than that of late evening. He could make things out. And it was quieter, too. The storm was passing. The ——

He could see somebody lying on the floor in the middle of the room. He could hear moans coming from whoever lay there. He hurled a jumble of broken things aside to reach the prostrate person.

A man. A man with his clothing torn and slashed, and with blood on the floor around him.

Eric shouted again; shouted, "Ann! Ann!"

There was no answer.

The storm was abating, but water still beat down on the house.

[160]

The wind was quieter, but it still rushed through the room. Probably Ann was upstairs. If he closed the window, closed out the sounds of the storm, she might hear him, might call back to him.

He pushed things aside to reach the window. He reached out and slammed it shut and then looked down.

Ann lay on the floor under the window. She lay entirely still. She lay face down.

Eric dropped to his knees beside her and called her name, not so loudly now. He reached for her and his hands felt the wetness of her clothing.

He looked at his shaking hands in the increasing light.

His hands were not red from her wet clothing. There was only water on his hands.

He lifted her up gently and held her up. There was little color in her face. His hands on her body sought the movement of her breathing.

XIII

THE STORM CLEARED Van Brunt at a little after seven and rumbled eastward, muttering sullen good-byes. Above the highlands across the Hudson the sun came out, slanting into the hilltop house which once had been a barn. The house, which had been almost dark, became bright although wind from the northwest still buffeted it. The lights came back on and were pale and meaningless in the bright room. Sunlight paled the fire, which had been leaping red and yellow in the fireplace.

Colonel remained in front of it with his forepaws stretched toward it. Once a situation is settled in Colonel's mind it is set there, as if in concrete. A fireplace is to lie in front of, especially when the out-of-doors is antagonistic. It does not much matter whether there is a fire in the fireplace.

At the moment there still was, although Susan and Merton had let it burn low. They sat beyond their dog and faced the fire, as he did. This was, Susan thought, another manifestation of the inertia to which humans as well as other animals are prone. The Heimrichs sipped drinks and Merton told his wife something about the way things were going in a village named North Wellwood.

The slanting sunshine reached the little black cat between Colonel's paws. The cat stood up, floated up. Then he arched his back. Then he sat down again, this time facing Colonel. He looked unblinkingly at the dog, his yellow eyes round, his pupils waning to slits. Then he said, "Muyah."

Colonel slightly opened one eye, but made no comment. He did move his right forepaw so that it touched the tiny cat and nudged him toward the other enormous paw.

"Colonel," Susan said, "is trying to tell the mite it's too early to get up."

The cat pounced on the paw which had moved. He rolled off the paw onto his back and used four feet on the paw, with the apparent intention of tearing it into pieces. Colonel made a low rumbling sound from somewhere in his throat, but he did not move his paw.

"Children can be so active," Susan said. "Delightful, of course, but sometimes tiring to their parents. Which reminds me." She looked at the watch on her wrist. "The Lathams thought about seven," she said. "But a storm like that knocks everything galley-west. What does galley-west mean, by the way? Where does it come from?"

"I haven't the faintest idea," Merton told her. "They're bringing the boy?"

"Their turn," Susan said.

The Lathams lived on Van Brunt Pass; they had a son of about the age of Michael Faye; the Latham boy was also on the high-school baseball team and today had been a day for practice. Mary Latham and Susan Heimrich alternated in the transportation of young ballplayers.

A car horn sounded twice outside. Susan floated up from her chair, rather as the tiny black cat had floated to his feet. She went very quickly to the door and out onto the terrace. She's been anxious, Heimrich thought. About her boy. About our boy. He heard the Latham car crunch on the turnaround and crunch away from it down the drive.

He's shooting up, Heimrich thought, watching his stepson open the door for Susan. He's almost as tall as his mother. He's skinny, but that's all right. He's got a good fast ball, from what I've seen of it.

"We've no idea where," Susan said over her shoulder to her son. "He just came home with it in his mouth. Michael's already eaten, Merton. They stopped somewhere to wait the rain out. Hamburgers, I suppose? With a lot of catsup?"

"Not really a lot, Mother," Michael said. "Good evening, Dad."

There was likely to be considerable formality in young Michael's speech. That had bothered them both a little. But "mother" is, in the opinion of both Heimrichs, better than "mom" and "dad" than "sir." It had taken young Michael several years to drop the "sir."

Colonel struggled to his feet when he heard god's voice. The tiny cat bristled at the movement; he seemed, for an instant, twice his minute size. He also hissed.

Colonel paid no attention to this. He shook stiffness out of his long legs and went toward god at what was, for him, a prance. He also wagged his entire rear end. In front of god he started to stand up on hind legs, intending to put paws on shoulders and wash a face. In outbursts of affection, Colonel is apt to knock people over.

"No, Colonel," Michael said. "Not tonight, Colonel."

Colonel, who had been halfway up, settled. He whimpered.

Young Michael scratched his dog behind both ears in recompense. He said, "Show me this cat of yours, Colonel."

And Colonel, to the complete astonishment of the three of them, turned away from god and pointed toward the little cat. And the cat jumped twice across the floor, each jump half a dozen times the length of cat, and landed on Colonel's left forepaw.

It was a blustery clear night when Heimrich, after dinner—young Michael found he could be persuaded, hamburgers or not, to eat a substantial piece of cake—went out to the garage. It was also a chilly night. Before the storm, the temperature had been in the low eighties. It was now, at a guess, in the mid-fifties and going down. Susan had planted tomato plants on Sunday. Mid-May was supposed to be safe in southern Putnam County, although some old residents held out for June. Old residents may be right, Heimrich thought, and shivered his way back into the house.

Colonel had followed god into god's bedroom, as was his right. The small black kitten was sitting on Susan's knee. The kitten clung and purred.

"He shinnied up," Susan said. "He shinnies very well, if a little like a lineman climbing a pole. With spikes." She looked at the big manila envelope under Heimrich's arm. She said, "Homework again?" and there was reproach in her voice. "I did hope that when you got to be an inspector." She finished with a quick shrug of slim shoulders. The cat said "Meyaaah," reproach in his small voice.

"Only a little," Heimrich said and took out of the envelope the canceled checks and bank statements Ray Crowley had put in the glove compartment of the Buick.

The little cat went down Susan's trousered leg, paw under paw. Susan said, "Ouch, Mite!" Mite crossed to Heimrich's leg and looked at it thoughtfully. Heimrich moved it out of range by crossing it over the other. The little cat said, "Yah" and sat in front of Heimrich and looked up at him. Then the cat seemed to be looking not at the man but beyond him and it seemed to Heimrich that there was an abstracted expression in the unblinking yellow eyes. It was, Heimrich thought, as if the cat were trying to remember something.

Then the little black cat said "Yow," with emphasis and turned away abruptly and trotted toward the kitchen, as if he had remembered an appointment there. After a moment there was a sound of scratching, claws on metal.

"Toilet pan," Susan said. "You put in something called, revoltingly I think, Klean Kitty. With *K*'s of course. Mite has known why, and where, the pan is since this morning."

"As a detective," Heimrich said, "I deduce we've got us a cat."

"I think so," Susan said. "We don't want to hurt Colonel's feelings, after the trouble he went to."

She stood up.

"I've got a book," she said. "Which is evidently just as well. Will you be long?"

"I shouldn't be," Heimrich told her. "Half an hour ought to do it."

The statements, with the canceled checks folded inside them, went back for two years. They showed quarterly deposits of three thousand dollars each and over the two years the monthly balance had not varied much. And the checks tended to repeat themselves—monthly checks to Brown's Market; smaller checks to Brown's Liquors; checks to a laundry and to a cleaner and to the Bennington Refuse Service. She had charged the gasoline for her car and paid by check. She had bought cordwood and paid telephone and electric bills and a doctor and a dentist. Until early in the current year she had sent monthly checks to a mortgage company.

There was nothing at all out of the ordinary in the statements Faith Powers had received from the First National Bank of North Wellwood. She had led a settled life and paid her bills, for the most part by the tenth of the month. She had lived within her means, which seemed to amount to twelve thousand a year plus a small monthly deposit which, at a guess, came from a pension fund.

Heimrich sat in front of what remained of the fire and gazed into it, without seeing it. The small black cat had curled up in a chair in front of the fire. It was very peaceful, except for the sound of the wind outside. It was also a little puzzling. It was not quite ten o'clock when the telephone bell jangled away the peace.

Heimrich went to the telephone and said, "Heimrich" and then, "Yes, Charlie."

"Somebody," Lieutenant Charles Forniss said, "has heaved a couple of hand grenades into the Martin house. Through an open window. That man from the network, Strothers, is still in the operating room at the Brewster hospital and he's full of shrapnel and maybe he'll make it and maybe he won't. Shrapnel missed Mrs. Martin but something hit her on the head and knocked her out. Looks like having been a small table. She'll be all right but they're keeping her overnight at the hospital, just to be sure. And whoever did it wrecked his car but got away on foot. For now, anyway. A dozen or so cruise cars are looking for him."

"When did it happen?" Heimrich asked him.

It had happened during the storm. It had been one hell of a storm. It had put the lights out—they were back now—and knocked down a lot of trees. It had been a good night to drive up to an isolated house and throw hand grenades into it—a wet night, but a good one for the purpose. If anybody heard the grenades go off they would figure it was a couple of cracks of thunder. If Eric Martin hadn't happened to be coming up the drive when the grenade thrower was trying to get out of it, and if the drive hadn't been narrow for two cars, whoever it was might have got away with it. As it happened . . .

Forniss told Heimrich what, as far as they had found out, had happened.

"Why no lights?"

Probably because the driver had thought he could more or less coast down the driveway and keep his lights off until he reached the road. It was dark, but not all that dark, and there was a lot of lightning. Perhaps, at the last minute, Martin's lights had blinded the fleeing man.

"Martin's all right?"

"Now that they say his wife is, or will be. Pretty wild before that. Particularly as this guy took a couple of potshots at him. Missed. Martin was behind his station wagon. One of the bullets went through the hood of the wagon. Then this guy . . ."

"Martin can't identify him?" Heimrich asked, after Forniss had finished.

"Small, he thinks," Forniss said. "Thin, anyway. Wearing a raincoat and it was blowing all around him. Everything was blowing all around everything just then. Certain he used a handgun, Martin is. Revolver, automatic. He couldn't be sure which. Revolver, probably, with only two shots, spaced out. The man had a hell of a lot of guns to choose from. In the car he wrecked."

There had been two shotguns in the car, and a semiautomatic rifle. There had been three hand grenades and a forty-five automatic in the glove compartment alone. There had also been a portable typewriter in the car. The weapons hadn't been touched, of course. The fingerprint boys were on their way from the Barracks.

"Car license?"

New York plates. Registered owner being checked on. No report as yet. No registration certificate in the glove compartment, but most car owners carry that in their pocket, along with their driver's permit.

"This man who ran from the car, after missing with a couple of shots," Heimrich said. "He wasn't carrying anything? Except probably a handgun? Under his raincoat, say?"

"Martin's pretty sure he wasn't. Is pretty sure he had both hands free and stuck the gun in his raincoat pocket while he was running. What would—oh."

"Yes, Charlie," Heimrich said. "There wasn't a twenty-two rifle in the car, was there? Quite an arsenal. Enough, say, for four men who wanted to do a lot of shooting. But no twenty-two."

"Four men," Forniss repeated and then added, "Yep. Could be. Only, the twenty-two could be in one of the other cars."

"Now, Charlie," Heimrich said. "Naturally. Only, it looks a bit as if they—we're guessing, but we have to guess, don't we?—had put all their eggs in one basket. Wouldn't you think? The headman's car, at a guess. The boss's car. The others—the fishermen, say—left earlier. Just innocent fishermen, with nothing but tackle in their cars. The boss had one more errand to run."

"Why Mrs. Martin, M.L.? And this guy Strothers?"

"Strothers had interviewed Nagle. Could identify him. But—a lot of other things. The documentary they made in Mississippi, or wherever. I didn't see it, but I gather it was about bigotry and racism. Right-wing violence, among other things. Call it an exposé. People like these Patriots United probably considered it part of the Communist conspiracy."

"The United Broadcasting Network?" There was incredulity in Forniss's voice.

"Man running for some office down there a while back called the New York *Times* a 'Socialist sheet,'" Heimrich said. "There was a witness in a trial of some Minutemen who said one of its cells had considered putting cyanide in the air-conditioning system at the United Nations. Sanity isn't involved, Charlie. Root out evil wherever found. With grenades. Beat a civil rights worker to death in his parsonage. And terrorize a village where there may be an interracial club. Scare off or kill off TV people who might dig into it. And might make the village ashamed to block the club."

"I'll buy that Nagle, if Pederson is Nagle, might go after a man who could identify him," Forniss said. "Nagle's wanted. Fugitive from justice. And he could have followed Strothers from the inn. Before the storm broke. The UBN car is easy enough to spot. Strothers did stop by the inn on his way to the Martin house. Made a reservation for tonight. And he and Mrs. Martin had been interviewing people. The whole town knows that."

"We'll ask Nagle when we find him," Heimrich said. "Which may take a bit of doing."

"Moon's up now," Forniss said. "Plenty of cruisers looking. And unmarked cars. Picked up four men already. Residents out for a walk. And looking at the damage the storm did. There's a train out of Brewster about now for New York. It's a long walk but maybe Nagle likes to walk. There's a car there. We'll need luck, yep. Of course, if he and these fishermen are in it together, one of them could have picked him up."

Heimrich doubted that. The fishermen had probably taken off; were holed in wherever their holes were. They had had no reason to think that Nagle would wreck his car and need a lift.

Heimrich said, "Where are you, Charlie?"

Forniss was at the substation. And ——

"Here're the fingerprint boys," he said. "Took them long enough. I'll call you back when ——"

"No," Inspector M. L. Heimrich said, "I'll come over, Charlie. It's a nice night for a drive."

Forniss said, "O.K., M.L."

There wasn't, of course, anything else he could say. He couldn't say, "If you think I'm not up to the job, take me off it." He couldn't say, as Heimrich said to himself, "When you delegate, delegate."

Forniss could hang up the receiver in the substation in North Wellwood, and that he did do.

"So you can't stop yourself," Susan said from the bedroom. She had, evidently, opened the door between the rooms when the telephone rang. "You're supposed to have a *desk* job, remember? D-E-S-K? And Charles Forniss is a good man. You don't have to hold his hand."

"I know," Heimrich said, and went into the bedroom. He looked down at his wife, who was wearing a nightgown he particularly liked and a filmy jacket over her shoulders and was lying in her bed and looking up at him.

"I love you very much," Susan said. "You are completely impossible. What can you do that Charlie can't do?"

"Nothing, probably," Heimrich said. "But I want to see a man about a gun."

He leaned over her and she put her arms around his neck and held him to her.

"A long time ago," Susan said. "Before we were married. I used to call you an 'oaf' in my mind. Did I ever say it?"

[170]

"No. Why? I mean, probably I am. But specifically?"

"You were very slow on the uptake," Susan said. "I love you very much, Merton. I'll change your ways tomorrow. That's from a song."

"I know," Merton Heimrich said.

"There ought to be a law against guns," Susan said. "Against all guns. We ought to go back to bows and arrows, if anything at all."

She watched him strap his shoulder holster on, and button his jacket over it. She held her arms out again and he lifted her up for a moment and held her against him, being careful about the thirty-two revolver on his chest.

"Take care," Susan said. "Bring yourself back alive." . . .

The moon was very bright and the wind still high. He turned the heater on in the car. The driveway had not washed badly. There was a large puddle at the foot of it, but nothing the Buick couldn't splash through.

It had much splashing to do on the way to North Wellwood. Once, after he had turned off the last main highway and onto one of Wellwood's side roads, Heimrich had to get out of the car and lug a heavy branch from the roadway. Twice he had to slow to creep around the trucks of repair crews stretching lines the storm had broken. It took an hour and a half to reach the substation.

"They've picked up a man near Brewster who's maybe the one we want," the trooper on duty told Heimrich. "He had a gun, anyway. They're holding him."

"The lieutenant?"

Forniss was at the Brewster hospital. Ann Martin had regained consciousness. Forniss had gone, with medical approval, to see what she remembered. "He left you this."

"This" was a typed five lines:

"M.L. Prints on shotgun and rifle check out. Pederson's on rifle and gun and typewriter; also on car. FP boys brought along photos of prints from rooms at inn. Fishermen also handled guns. Nothing in from Washington on print ident. Mrs. Martin conscious; gone to see. C.F."

The telephone rang on the trooper's desk, behind which he was, in deference to rank, standing. He picked the telephone up and said, "State police, Trooper Bartoni" and listened and said, "Yes he is, Professor. One moment," and reached the telephone out toward Heimrich and said, "Professor Brinkley, Inspector."

"Your Susan said you might be there," Brinkley said. He sounded rather excited. "I am afraid I waked her up, Merton. Probably it isn't really important, but I thought it might have some bearing. The club's going to get its permit. The zoning board had a special meeting this evening and decided that, and Sam Bennington telephoned Clay Foster. To get the story in this week's edition. And Clay, thinking I'd be interested—quite rightly, Merton, quite rightly —telephoned me. And I thought you might be and—I suppose the phrase is—tracked you down. I do hope I didn't worry Susan."

"I'm afraid she's used to it," Heimrich said. "And I am interested that the club's permit's gone through. Rather sudden decision, wasn't it?"

"Quite," Walter Brinkley said. "Quite sudden. Oh, and by the way, Merton. Somebody's stolen my car."

XIV

ANN MARTIN SAID she was perfectly all right, except for a headache, and that she did not want to stay overnight in the hospital. She said there was no sense to it. She said she wanted to go home. Eric Martin, sitting beside her bed—and looking rather more harried than she did—said, "Nonsense, dear. You'll do as you're told." Then he looked up at Forniss, who was standing on the other side of the bed. He said, "You've got what you want? You can leave her alone now?"

"If that's all she remembers, yes," Forniss said. "You didn't see anybody. Just an object in the air coming through the window. Then an explosion and then another object. That's the size of it?"

"She's told you that," Eric Martin said. He was a very cross man, Forniss thought. Understandably enough, on the whole. A man who comes home in a storm, is almost run down by another car and is shot at; a man who finds an acquaintance lying in blood on the floor of a blasted living room and his wife unconscious under an open window—such a man may well be cross.

"Yep," Forniss said. "She has, Mr. Martin. One other thing, Mrs. Martin, and I'll let you get some sleep. Do you think the network will go ahead with a—what do you call it? A documentary about this club business?"

"I don't know. It's—oh, it's so much spot news now. What with the blowing up of the newspaper and now this—this blowing up of Roy and me. Lieutenant, is Roy *really* going to be all right?"

"The doctors say so," Forniss told her. "Not as badly hurt as he looked at first. Seems he dropped down behind a chair when he heard the grenade hit the floor and the chair took most of it. In the recovery room now, Mr. Strothers is. Probably out from under the anesthetic. And ——"

Somebody knocked on the door of the hospital room and then

opened it. A nurse came in and said, "How are we, Mrs. Martin?" and then, without waiting to be told how they were, said, "You're wanted on the telephone, Lieutenant Forniss."

Ann and Eric watched Forniss go. They watched the nurse stay. She was a stern nurse; she looked sternly at Eric Martin. "We," she said, "must get our sleep."

Ann was propped up in the hospital bed; propped so she could see Eric's face. It was a face she was learning to know. She watched it tighten in a way she knew.

"If you're so sleepy," Eric said up to the firm nurse, "why don't you ——"

"No, dear," Ann said. "She's right, really. If all of you won't let me go home."

"You hear the little lady, Mr. Martin," the nurse said. "We'll have something to make us sleep, won't we, dear?"

Ann looked at her husband's face. She saw the tightness ebb out of it slowly.

Eric stood up. He said, "I suppose so. But the first thing tomorrow we'll go home. Really go home. Back where we belong."

He leaned down toward her. The nurse went to the window and looked out it. Even her tact was firm.

Ann looked up at Eric and then slowly and carefully shook her head. She said, "Ouch!" Then she said, "If you mean go back to New York, darling ——" And then, even more carefully, she moved her head from side to side on the pillows.

Eric Martin stood up and looked down at his wife and for the moment he seemed as stern as the nurse.

"You," Eric told his wife, "must be crazy. You don't mean—damn it, you *can't* mean—after all this ——"

"Yes, darling," Ann said. "I think I do. We don't want to be pushed around, do we? Pushed out?"

"For all I care," Eric said. "They ——" But he broke off there and looked down at her, now with wonderment. When he continued, he spoke slowly, each word a careful word.

"Do you," he said, "really mean you want to stay here? Where

[174]

people throw hand grenades at other people? Where —— My God, darling! Anyway, the house is a wreck."

"We'll have somebody put it back together," Ann said. "It was probably all insured. We'll pick out the furniture ourselves to take the place of whatever is broken. We'll get things we like. Things we'll like to live with. We'll ——"

"You sound," Eric said, and still made each word a careful word, "as if, after all this, we were going to live in North Wellwood." He paused and shook his head, rather hopelessly. "As if," he said, "we were going to exercise our option to buy."

"Do I, dear? Perhaps I do. Not only because we don't want to be pushed around. Because, Eric, I think we'll like it in the village. If the tempest has blown out in the teacup."

The man they were holding at the Brewster substation was a dark and narrow man—long-faced and with a nose rather like a scimitar splitting it. He had deep-set black eyes and black hair and he wanted a lawyer. It was outrageous that he was being held and of course he had a permit for the .32-calibre Smith & Wesson in the pocket of his raincoat. Didn't happen to have it with him. His name wasn't Pederson. His name certainly wasn't Aaron Nagle. His name was Johannes Schmidt and he was a piano player. He'd never been in North Wellwood in his life. He'd been in Brewster at a friend's house for dinner. He was a patriotic American citizen.

The last statement did not, to Lieutenant Forniss, seem particularly relevant. The .32 Smith & Wesson, with no permit forthcoming, did. Violation of the state law against the carrying of concealed weapons. Which would do for a start.

"Traffic violation too," the trooper sergeant told Forniss.

The narrow man had driven up to the Brewster railroad station in an MG. He had run it into an area reserved for taxicabs and jumped out of it and started for the last train to New York, which was at the station, its Diesels breathing heavily. He had been at the steps of the second of the train's two cars when a uniformed trooper said, "Hold it a minute, mister. Want to talk to you."

[175]

The narrow man had turned abruptly and tried to run back to the MG. He had got only a couple of steps.

"Didn't hear me?" the trooper said, and held him. "Said I wanted to talk to you. Guess we'll make it back at the substation."

He slapped the narrow man's pockets and said, "Well, well," and took the revolver out of the right-hand raincoat pocket and put it in a pocket of his own. He had driven the narrow man back to the substation, which was not far. "Could be the one we're looking for," the trooper told the sergeant. It was then the narrow man began talking about his right to a lawyer.

Forniss used the telephone.

"Oughtn't to let you," the hospital physician said. "Lost a bit of blood—hell, quite a lot of blood. Under mild sedation. Fighting it, though. Some of them do."

"Tell him to keep on fighting it," Forniss said. "Won't be ten minutes. Won't—shouldn't—take more than a few seconds. O.K.?"

Reluctantly, the resident physician supposed so.

Roy Strothers was out of the recovery room and in a private room at the hospital. He was propped up in the bed. Both arms were heavily bandaged and his head was bandaged. But his eyes were uncovered and open when Forniss propelled the thin man into the room, with the resident and a nurse behind them.

"Know this man?" Forniss said. "One word will do."

Strothers's voice was low and had a crack in it. But it was steady and he did not hesitate.

"Yes," Strothers said. "Hello, Nagle, you rat." He did not move his head, but he moved his eyes toward Forniss. "He the one who plays with hand grenades?"

"Yep," Forniss said. "Could be, Mr. Strothers. You can go to sleep now."

Forniss took the narrow man, who had said nothing in the hospital room, back to the substation.

"You can add fugitive from justice to the charges," Forniss told the sergeant. "And suspicion of assault with a deadly weapon."

"I want a lawyer," the narrow man said. "It's my constitutional right to have a lawyer. We've got that much left of it. In spite of what the Commies in Washington. I ——"

"From the Barracks you can call a lawyer," Forniss told him. "You'll have plenty of time, Mr. Nagle."

Walter Brinkley thought the threat of a TV invasion of North Wellwood had forced the board's hand. Sam Bennington hadn't said as much to Clayton Foster, but Foster thought he had said almost that much.

"A washing of dirty linen in public," Brinkley said. "It might have come to something like that, Merton. A way to stop that would be to wash the linen in private first. For the good name of the community. I've no idea how these things work, but I'd think granting the permit would take the wind out of the network's sails. In my dotage I no longer care too much about a mixing of metaphors."

They were in the living room of Brinkley's house on Hayride Lane. Heimrich used a finger to circle ice in an old-fashioned glass which had a very little bourbon in it. Walter Brinkley, after urging a nightcap on his friend, had himself elected milk, with a little rum in it.

"Foster thinks that was what decided them?" Heimrich asked him.

Foster did; had told Brinkley he did. As an effort to protect the community's good name. "What's left of it," Brinkley said and shook his head and sipped milk with a little rum in it. "Already, I'm afraid, we sound like a violent people. Intolerant, uncontrolled." He sighed. "Archaic in attitude," he said. "Will Mrs. Martin be all right? And this man Strothers?"

Mrs. Martin certainly, Heimrich told him. Strothers, from last reports—Heimrich had checked before he left the substation—probably would be all right. A bit scarred up, but all right.

"What the Martins must think of our town," Brinkley said. "What they must think, Merton."

He shook his head again, and sighed again.

"Probably they don't think much of it," Heimrich said. "The community hasn't spread the welcome mat, exactly. Tell me about your car, Walter."

[177]

The MG had been taken out of the garage just as the storm was passing. Brinkley had heard nothing. "But there was still a lot of thunder." When the rain slackened, he had gone out to close the garage door. "After the horse was stolen," Brinkley said. "My night for bromides."

Brinkley had gone back into the house to report the theft of his car but had gone in to hear the telephone ringing. It had been Foster to tell him of the sudden decision of the zoning board. And while Foster was on the telephone, just as he was finishing his account and his speculations, another telephone in the *Sentinel* office had rung and he had said, "Wait a minute, Walter" and gone to answer it. He had come back and said, "More hell's broken loose. Somebody's bombed the Martins."

"So," Walter Brinkley told Heimrich, "I decided the police had enough to do, for the moment, without my bothering them. It's really quite an old car. Lately it's taken to stalling at the most inopportune moments."

Did he happen to remember the license number?

"Of course not, Merton. Does anyone, really? But it must be around some place. I'm quite sure it must be. Unless, of course, I left it in the glove compartment. I'll ——"

He put his glass down on the table with a blink and bounced out of his chair and into the hall and up the stairs. He bounced down after several minutes and waved a billfold as if it were a flag.

"Right where I thought it was," Walter Brinkley said in triumph but also, Heimrich thought, somewhat in surprise.

The registration certificate was in the billfold and this, also, seemed to surprise Walter Brinkley.

Heimrich called the local substation. He was on for several minutes before he came back to tell Brinkley his car was in Brewster and would be brought back as soon as someone was free to bring it back.

"A getaway car," Brinkley said. "Think of that."

There was pleasure in Walter Brinkley's voice. Once, some years before, he had been involved—*personally* involved—in one of his friend's cases. It had been unpleasant, of course. It had been shocking. But it had been exciting. Having his car stolen as a getaway car wasn't anything like that. Still, it was something . . .

I can, Heimrich thought, driving back in the moonlight toward North Wellwood center, go on to the Barracks and sit in on the questioning of Aaron Nagle, wanted in Missouri for murder. Which would come first, of course. Assault with a deadly weapon, violation of the Sullivan law, grand larceny—all these are serious enough matters but all of them, even lumped together, come after murder. And, naturally, if Missouri slipped up on it, they could always haul Mr. Nagle back to New York.

But if I go to the Barracks and sit in, Heimrich thought, I'll be superseding Charlie—once more superseding Charlie. I assign him to a case and the case is his. Ought to be his. Damn it all, *is* his. And it's too late at night now to do what, primarily, I came here to do. Anyway, that too is Charlie's. I'll go home now and in the morning I'll go to my desk at the Barracks, and tomorrow—all of tomorrow—I'll sit at it. And delegate.

For no special reason, except that the house Faith Powers had lived in was part of what he had horned in on, was now horning out of, Heimrich slowed when he was abreast of the house. Then, opposite the driveway, he stopped the Buick and looked up the drive at the house, which was white in the moonlight. And in front of which, standing black in the moonlight, there was a car.

Moonlight plays tricks. It is mirrored on windows and the shadows of leaves move in it, so that its reflection flickers. There was no way of being sure, without driving up to see, whether somebody really was using a flashlight to prowl Faith Powers's house. Using a pocket light after the electricity had come back into the wires? Of course, sometimes after a storm one house will remain dark after the others come alight. Sometimes one transformer burns out beyond recovery. Still . . .

Heimrich backed the Buick until he could turn up the drive. When he was just in it, he switched off his lights. He could see the rest of the way by moonlight.

He did not drive the rest of the way. Halfway up the drive he stopped the car and got out and walked toward the big house, which looked so much bigger in the moonlight. He left the Buick to block the drive.

The car in front of the house was big, too, in the moonlight. It was a Lincoln Continental, big in any light. Heimrich reached into his pocket for a flashlight, felt its hard roundness and decided there was, for the moment, enough light without it. He leaned down and read the numbers on the license plate of the Continental and tucked the numbers into his memory. He stayed for a moment crouched in the car's black shadow and looked at the house.

He saw nothing at first. The moonlit windows stared at him blankly. But then, behind one of them—a window which would, at a guess, be on the left of a central entrance hall—there was, briefly, the moving beam of a flashlight. A fairly powerful light. It was not being pointed at the window, but away from it.

Heimrich went from the car's shadow into a strip of moonlight between car and house. On the porch of the house he was again in darkness. The porch flooring creaked when he stepped on it, which was unfortunate. He stood motionless for some seconds and listened and heard nothing. Then he tried the door.

It was not locked, and he opened it slowly. A faint click of the latch could not be avoided. But the door did not creak as he pushed it open.

Inside, he felt for a light switch where, on the right of the door, it would most likely be. His fingers found it. The switch lever was down. Unless it was a three-way switch, that meant that whoever was prowling the house had not wanted more light than a flashlight would supply. Had not probably wanted light which would be seen from the road.

If the prowler had been listening, and prowlers ought to listen, he had by now heard Heimrich on the porch. Or heard the Buick in the driveway before Heimrich cut the engine. Or seen me, Heimrich thought, as I walked up in the moonlight. So I'm not going to surprise him. I may as well have lights on things.

He flicked the light switch up. And nothing happened.

The transformer which served the house, this single house, had burned out, probably. Or a surge of electricity through wires had burned a house fuse or tripped a main circuit breaker.

Heimrich took his flashlight out of his pocket. He did not immediately turn it on. He stood and listened.

The room on the left of the central hall had windows on the moon's side. The door to it was open and moonlight lay on the floor inside. Heimrich waited. There was no sound from the room.

Then a black shadow moved on the lighted floor and, as it moved, Heimrich could hear the footfalls of the man who made it. The prowler had decided to make a break for it.

The beam leaped from Heimrich's flashlight and he ran across the hall. He ran into the room and heard a door close hard and was in an empty room. The closed door was at the end of the room.

Heimrich swung the beam from his flashlight around the room. The walls were lined with books. Near one of the windows there was a desk and the drawers of the desk were open. There was a small filing cabinet beside the desk and its single drawer gaped open.

Where Ray Crowley had found checkbook and passbook and bank statements? Probably. Where a prowler had been looking for them? That, too, was probable. For such financial records and for something else?

Heimrich's mind worked and his legs worked. He was across the room, yanking open the door. He sent the light's beam along a short corridor which led toward the rear of the house. The corridor was empty. It ended at a closed door.

Heimrich ran the length of it, not trying to run silently. There was no longer any sense in that. At the door he stopped abruptly and then turned back. He had passed a closed door on his right. He went back to the door and opened it, turning the knob with his left hand, which also held the flashlight. He might need his right hand.

The door opened to a bathroom. The bathroom was empty.

He had wasted seconds. But a prowler could have dodged into the bathroom and, when pursuit had passed, dodged out of it again.

The door at the end of the corridor opened into a pantry, with a kitchen beyond it. There was a swinging door in the right wall of the pantry. It was not swinging.

On the far side of the kitchen there was a closed door. Already out that way? If that way was a way to the open? Or through the swinging door into, at a guess, a dining room? Heimrich stood in the middle of the kitchen, in moonlight up to his knees, and listened.

He heard wind against the house. He heard the sounds a house makes by itself, alone in the night and the temperature changing. From above him there was a cracking sound. But it was a single sound, sharper and quicker than a man's feet would make. And it seemed unlikely that the prowler would have fled upstairs.

The prowler, Heimrich thought, probably knows this house well —knows how corridors led into rooms and rooms into other rooms. From the size of it, this could be a labyrinth of a house; could be a house to get lost in. Was the prowler holed up somewhere, waiting for pursuit to blunder? As, Heimrich thought gloomily, it was certainly blundering now. It was pursuit at a standstill. And, come to think of it, very visible in the moonlight from a kitchen window. Heimrich moved out of the moonlight. There was no special reason to think the prowler had a gun with him. There was, on the other hand, no special reason to think he hadn't.

Heimrich, making as little noise as he could manage, went to the kitchen door and looked out at an empty yard with moonlight on it. The door was locked. More than that. The door was bolted on the inside. Which answered one question, for what it was worth.

He went back to the pantry and pushed open the swinging door and went into a dining room. There was a round table in the center of it, and four chairs arranged around the table and there were other chairs set against the walls. There was a closed door at the far end of the room and Heimrich walked toward it.

And then, when he was some distance from it, he heard the sound of heavily running feet and, in an instant, the slamming of a door. The sounds came from the front of the house.

Heimrich yanked at the dining-room door and it was locked. From the other side. It takes only an instant to turn a key in a lock. A locked door slows pursuit.

Heimrich went back through the dining room, the beam of his

[182]

flashlight bouncing on the floor. He went into the pantry and along the corridor and into the book-lined room. The door from it to the central hall was closed. I left it open, Heimrich thought, and tried it. The prowler hadn't missed that, either.

Back through the kitchen and out the kitchen door and around the house and ——

The starter of a car whined harshly. Heimrich jumped to a front window of the library, and looked out at the drive. As he pulled the window up the lights of the big Continental went on. The big car jerked backward and then jumped forward down the driveway the Buick blocked.

The big car slowed when its lights picked up the blocking car. The driveway was a little depressed there. The Continental tilted as it went off onto the grass around the Buick but it did not tilt too much.

Heimrich went out through the window, which seemed quicker. Not that there was any great hurry now. He took time to run the flashlight beam up and down the furrows the Continental had made in wet sod. Good tread prints. The technical boys would be pleased with them.

Heimrich backed the Buick toward the road. He had to be careful in swinging, because a truck of the New York Electric and Gas Corporation was parked on the other side of the road. A man was up a pole, doing something to the transformer. Electricity would soon be available to an empty house.

Heimrich drove toward North Wellwood center on Hayride Lane. But when he reached its intersection with South Lane he turned right. After a few hundred yards he turned left and was on Long Hill Road. He didn't hurry. He did look for a big car which might be parked by the roadside, its lights off.

As it had been, perhaps, the night before? Farther along the road, then, and on the other side of it? Heimrich rather doubted it had been. Big cars show up in moonlight.

Names on mailboxes show up in the lights of a car. Heimrich turned the Buick up a driveway. Again, he did not drive on to a house, and again he cut his lights when he was in the drive. Again he left the Buick to block the drive. Again he walked in the moonlight, which was unavoidable. He kept to the side of the drive and was part of the time in the black shadows of trees. But there were patches of moonlight he had to walk through.

There were lights behind two upstairs windows in this house.

One of the doors of a two-car garage was open. The garage had its back to the moon and it cast a black shadow. Heimrich walked into the darkness of the garage—into the stall which held a big car.

He had to use his flashlight to read the license plate. He walked to the front of the car and felt the hood. Not that he needed to, but he might sometime have to swear in court that he had felt the hood. And found it warm.

He walked out into the moonlight. There was no other place to walk.

There was a flash from the porch of the house he started toward and the crack of a rifle and, behind him, the thud of a bullet into the closed door of the garage. The bullet whined at Heimrich as it passed him.

Heimrich got his gun out and yelled, "Police!" and raised the revolver.

The man on the porch of the house fired again and this time the bullet came close enough to Heimrich to hiss at him.

Heimrich fired a shot, but fired it into the air.

Then the whole area—the porch, the turnaround, the garage—was flooded with light from above.

The man with the rifle, it lowered now, came down shallow steps from the porch and said, "My God, Inspector. I might have hit you."

"Yes, Mr. Finch," Heimrich said, and walked on toward the big man who now stood at the foot of the shallow flight to the porch. "You might have at that. Do you always shoot first and ask afterwards?"

"Heard somebody in the garage," Lawrence Finch said. "My God, I'm glad I missed. Wasn't actually shooting to hit, you know. Just to scare off a prowler. If I'd wanted to hit ——" He shrugged his shoulders.

"Yes," Heimrich said. "I made quite a target in the moonlight.

[184]

And you only miss when you want to, don't you? Put the gun down, Mr. Finch. I'm a fairly good shot myself."

And he waggled his revolver back and forth.

Finch put the rifle down on the ground.

"A man has a right to protect his property," Finch said. "They haven't taken that away from us yet. Damn near everything else, but not that. I hear somebody getting ready to steal my car and ——"

"Naturally," Heimrich said. "Defend your home. Sure. Did you find what you were looking for in the Powers house, Mr. Finch? Let's go inside, shall we? We've got a bit of talking to do. Windy out here. No use yelling at each other over the wind."

Inside, Finch did not deny he had been at the Powers house. He did deny there was anything surreptitious about it.

"I'm the executor," he said. "Some papers I wanted. As her executor, I had a key."

He had gone over after power came back to North Wellwood. But it hadn't come back to the Powers house, so he used a flashlight. And . . .

"I was just about to call the police. Report that there was somebody in the house—somebody looking for what he could find to steal. I heard him banging around and figured if I came home and called up maybe you people'd be able to catch him."

"You hadn't called yet, I gather?"

"Just going to when I heard you in the gar——" He stopped and snapped his fingers. He said he'd be damned. "It was *you* in the house," he said. "Saw a light, I suppose and—I will be damned. Followed me here, thinking *you* were following a burglar."

Finch laughed. He said it was a damn funny mixup.

Heimrich did not laugh. He said, "Again, Mr. Finch. Did you find what you were looking for? Her bank records, perhaps? We've got those, Mr. Finch. Been over them, naturally. Nothing much that helps. Probably she had another checking account. In the city, perhaps. Used it to deposit these considerable sums she got from your selling her bonds for her."

"The deposits don't show on her account in the First National?"

"No, Mr. Finch."

"Then she must have had another account," Finch said. "One of the things I'll have to find out, as the executor of her estate."

"Started to try to find out tonight, I suppose," Heimrich said. "Very diligent of you. Didn't have any luck, I gather. Or was it something else you were looking for, Mr. Finch?"

Finch shook his head, a man bemused.

A detective has to follow hunches, make his stabs in the dark.

"Like," Heimrich said, "the letter you wrote her? Making an appointment for Monday night. Only, leaving the time up to her. Which was why she called you from the inn, wasn't it?"

"You're crazy," Finch said, and his voice went up. "I didn't write her any such ——"

"Now, Mr. Finch. You did, you know. Happens we've got it along with ——"

Finch interrupted him by jumping to his feet and by laughing—laughing loudly, almost hysterically.

"The hell you've got it," he said. "You think I'd leave ——"

And then, only then, he seemed to hear what he was shouting at a man who sat less than six feet from him.

He started to run toward the living-room door which opened to the entrance hall—and toward the front door and a rifle lying outside it on the ground. At least that was Heimrich's hunch. A detective has to follow his hunches.

Finch moved well for so big and soft a man. But Merton Heimrich was bigger and not soft at all. He caught Lawrence Finch in the entrance hall.

Finch swung at him. Heimrich had to knock him down. He used only the force necessary to subdue a man resisting arrest. The New York State Police try to be scrupulous in such matters.

XV

It was warm again by Saturday—terrace-warm at the Heimrich house on its hill above the Hudson. It was a day, for Susan, for shorts. Merton Heimrich, who considers himself ungainly for shorts, wore a blue polo shirt and gray slacks and no gun. He was off-duty for the day and for the next day. At least, that was to be hoped for.

Colonel lay in the shade, resting his tongue outside. His duties as a parent had, during the morning, been arduous. The small black cat, after a time of playing with Colonel's tail, had wandered off and had had to be found. Mite was in sight now. He was stalking something—something invisible except to his own yellow eyes. He stalked his own illusion through the grass. Young Michael had been picked up to pitch a ball game.

Susan and Merton Heimrich sipped pre-lunch drinks. And, as was inevitable, the telephone rang in the house. Susan said, "Damn!" which was equally inevitable. She said, "I'll get," but Heimrich was already on his way across the terrace.

He was gone for almost ten minutes, but when he walked back to their spot of shade and peace on the terrace, he smiled and shook his head. Which meant that, still, he was off-duty.

"Charlie," he said. "The Missouri State Police are very pleased with us. The Governor of Missouri is in the process of saying to the Governor of New York that they want Aaron Nagle, alias Harry Pederson. They're pleased, out there, because the threatening letters to a minister somebody beat to death were written on a portable typewriter we found for them in a car with Nagle's fingerprints widely distributed."

Nagle denied that he had had any part in the murder of a clergyman in southern Missouri, which was to be expected. For a time he had denied everything, including that he was Aaron Nagle, ex-educator, ex-American Nazi, present executive of Patriots United.

[187]

I

"Charlie talked to him," Heimrich told Susan. "Charlie and an assistant district attorney from White Plains."

A lawyer had been present; the lawyer had advised—had, as was to be expected, advised complete silence. Beyond denials. For a time he had got it, or something like it. Then . . .

"Since you just happened to be in North Wellwood," Charles Forniss said. "Doing your writing. With no interest in what was going on. Since it was that way, you won't be interested in the fact that the club got its permit."

And then, rather to the surprise of everyone and entirely to the indignation of Nagle's lawyer, Aaron Nagle had blown up. He had ranted; for more than a quarter of an hour he had shouted at them, gesticulated at them; called them—all of them—part of the Communist conspiracy. The conspiracy had taken over North Wellwood. "Reds. Niggers. Jews. Moscow. The Commies in Washington. The betrayal of the Constitution. The . . ."

Words tumbled out of Aaron Nagle—violent words; a jumble of violent words. He became incoherent with his violent words, and the lawyer, finally, had looked at the others and shrugged hopelessly and not tried to stop his client.

"Probably," Heimrich said, speaking relaxedly on the terrace above the Hudson, "if Nagle gets away with it out West and we get him back—for arson and attempted murder and, for that matter, illegal parking in Brewster ——" He stopped and sipped from his drink and looked down at the distant, shining river. He closed his eyes.

"If," Susan Heimrich said, "you'd really rather go to sleep."

"If," Merton Heimrich said, "we get him back and he gets the same lawyer, the plea probably will be not guilty by reason of insanity. I doubt if we'll get him back. I think Charlie has given the State of Missouri a wrapped-up package."

"I do realize, darling," Susan said, "that you had nothing to do with any of it. That you delegated it all to Charlie and sat properly at your desk. Barring, of course, the night you got yourself shot at. And chased Mr. Finch through an empty house and finally had to knock him out."

"Now, Susan," Heimrich said, "down. Not out."

[188]

"And guessed he had written a letter to Mrs. Powers, asking her to come and see him and to call to fix a time. And tricked him into admitting that he had written that letter and had got it and destroyed it. After he killed Mrs. Powers, of course. Got it at her house?"

"Probably. And also found and destroyed a list of securities which she had just begun to realize she didn't own because Finch had sold them, using the power of attorney she had given him a year or so ago when she went abroad. Used the money to buy land. A simple case of embezzlement, to begin with. Which, now Charlie knows what to look for, he won't have any great difficulty in proving."

"How did she find out what was going on?"

"We don't know," Heimrich said. "Maybe we'll never know. She probably wanted cash to invest in the club. He stalled her off. Ann Martin says that when she and Faith Powers were having lunch at the inn and Finch stopped by their table she had a feeling that Finch was stalling about something. The guess—Charlie's assumption, anyway—is that Faith got suspicious because of his stalling. And this we do know, she had, a few days before, gone to the town hall and looked over land records. The town clerk will testify to that. And he'll testify that she was interested in Finch's ownings. There'll be a lot of bits and pieces for Charlie to put together. There always are. It's not too difficult after we know what we've got to look for. After we got our break—Charlie got his break. In, as it turned out, a fairly literal fashion."

"If," Susan said, "you're going to be cryptic I think we might have another drink."

Merton Heimrich got to his feet. So, more laboriously, did Colonel. There was always something experimental about Colonel's arising; it was rather as if he were putting his long legs together for the first time. He stood and looked around the terrace and around the lawn stretching beyond it. He turned and looked at Susan and, a little querulously, woofed.

"I don't see him, either," Susan told the big dog. "But I'm sure your cat's around somewhere, Colonel. He's a competent little cat."

Colonel woofed again. There was no conviction in his woof. He walked off across the lawn toward the trees which bordered it.

Heimrich brought their drinks and put them within reach.

Susan sipped from hers. She said, "All right, darling. Break's the word."

"Of," Heimrich told her, "Faith Powers's right index finger. The finger she would have used to dial a telephone number with. As most right-handed people do."

"I," Susan said, "use a pencil. Better for the nails. But all right. So?"

So, instead of dialing Finch's number on the night she was killed, Faith Powers had used another finger to dial the operator. And the operator had helpfully dialed Finch's number for her.

"The real break was that the operator she got happened to be a local girl—a girl who knew her and knew her voice. And, being a local girl, knew Lawrence Finch's telephone number. And, being a retentive girl, remembers the incident."

"So that was how, when you said you wanted to see a man about a gun, you were pretty sure who the man was."

"Whoever murdered her, shot at Peters, used a twenty-two. There wasn't any twenty-two in Nagle's armament—damn near everything else, but no twenty-two."

"There wasn't any real connection between what Nagle was up to and what Finch did?"

"Now, Susan. Yes, probably there was. Finch knew that Nagle was in town, and what he was in town for—to make a demonstration against the club. He knew because Nagle got in touch with a contractor named Amos Smithton who had been publicly violent about the club. And who has two loutish sons, who, the village police suspected, had been sicked on the Martins by their father.

"Smithton passed the word on to Finch. He says casually, when they were arranging for a couple of loads of gravel."

Finch thought he had a cover. That would, at any rate, be contended when he came to trial for murder. Anything done against anybody who advocated the club would be blamed—Finch hoped it would be blamed—on Patriots United.

"If we didn't catch up with them," Heimrich said, "he probably would have pointed a finger at them."

He had taken two shots at Peters, not planning to hit him, to start what he hoped would be taken for a pattern—a pattern of impersonal violence, directed against Negroes and Communists. He believed that the shooting of Faith Powers would be taken as part of that pattern, since she was openly in favor of the club.

"He should have used a hand grenade."

"Naturally. Didn't have one handy. Also, he's a rifleman. Member of a rifle club. Thinks in terms of rifles."

"In her house? The night he shot at you. Did he, by the way, plan to miss you, too?"

"Probably. When he saw who I was and that I had a gun of my own. In her house? You mean, what was he after?"

"Naturally, darling."

"Her bank records. Which didn't show what they should have shown. Which, of course, he should have taken the first time round. Probably he didn't because he thought their absence would be more suspicious than their presence. Changed his mind when we showed interest in her finances."

"The bank could have duplicated them."

"Yes, Susan. If we'd guessed there was a discrepancy worth checking on. I suppose he thought that, without her statements to set us off, the idea of checking with the bank might not occur to us. To Charlie, that is."

"Of course to Charlie," Susan said. "Who else, dear? I do realize it was always Charlie's case and that you ——"

Barking interrupted her. It was barking to match the size of the dog who made it—and who, with a great loping, came toward them across the grass. At the edge of the terrace Colonel stopped, skidding a little. He looked from one to the other and woofed at each, and there was anxious urgency in his woofing. He turned as if to go back the way he had come, but stopped and looked back, alternatively, over his shoulders.

They went as their dog directed. With each step he looked back to make certain. They reassured him as he led them toward the trees which bordered their lawn.

There was a clump of trees and he led them into it. He came to the base of a tall ash and reared himself up against it and barked up it.

From a rather high crotch, Mite looked down at them. He was very small and very black in the big tree. When he was sure he had been seen, he made a plaintive sound down to them. Colonel barked back; he turned to Susan and Merton and whimpered.

"I know, Colonel," Susan Heimrich said gently to her dog. "It does seem unnatural to climb trees. But cats will do it, Colonel. You mustn't worry so. He'll come back down when he's ready."

Mite wasn't ready for almost an hour. But he did come down to join his family on the terrace. Colonel licked him to make sure. Mite was tolerant.